As Old as Cain

KENDELL FOSTER CROSSEN
Writing as
M.E. CHABER

STEEGER BOOKS / **2020**

PUBLISHED BY STEEGER BOOKS
Visit steegerbooks.com for more books like this.

PUBLISHING HISTORY

Hardcover
New York: Henry Holt & Co. (A Novel of Suspense), October 1954.
Toronto: George J. McLeod, 1954.

Paperback
New York: Mercury Publications, Bestseller Mystery #B202, 1957, as *Take One for Murder*. Paperback. Cover design by George Salter.
New York: Paperback Library (63-527), A Milo March Mystery, #17, February 1971. Cover by Robert McGinnis.

ISBN: 978-1-61827-506-6

Milo March is a hard-drinking, womanizing, wisecracking, James-Bondian character. He always comes out on top through a combination of personality, bluff, bravado, luck, skill, experience, and intellect. He is a shrewd judge of human character, a crack shot, and a deeper character than I have found in most of the other spy/thriller novels I've read. But, above all, he is a con-man—and a very good one. It is Milo March himself who makes the series worth reading.

—Don Miller, *The Mystery Nook* fanzine 12

Steeger Books is proud to reissue twenty-three vintage novels and stories by M.E. Chaber, whose Milo March Mysteries deliver mile-a-minute action and breezily readable entertainment for thriller buffs.

Milo is an Insurance Investigator who takes on the tough cases. Organized crime, grand theft, arson, suspicious disappearances, murders, and millions and millions of dollars—whatever it is, Milo is just the man for the job. Or even the only man for it.

During World War II, Milo was assigned to the OSS and later the CIA. Now in the Army Reserves, with the rank of Major, he is recalled for special jobs behind the Iron Curtain. As an agent, he chops necks, trusses men like chickens to steal their uniforms, shoots point blank at secret police—yet shows compassion to an agent from the other side.

Whatever Milo does, he knows how to do it right. When the work is completed, he returns to his favorite things: women, booze, and good food, more or less in that order....

THE MILO MARCH MYSTERIES

For Martha

No winter shall abate the spring's increase.
—John Donne

CONTENTS

AUTHOR'S NOTE

With the exception of Moses Hewit, Jesse Grant, Jesse West, John Goodman, William Poage, Eli Terry, Thomas Affleck, Thomas Tufft, Nicholas Disbrowe, Casper Wistar, John Frederick Amelung, John Hull, and Paul Revere, all characters in this novel are fictitious and are not intended to resemble any person, living or dead. Athens, Ohio, is a very real place, and I apologize for disturbing its tranquillity with even an imaginary murder.

M.E.C.

INT. LOG CABIN — NIGHT

59 CLOSE SHOT MARY

as she writes in her diary. CAMERA ANGLE shows open diary on desk, old lamp, Mary's hand as she writes in diary with quill pen. CAMERA MOVES IN until we can see writing.

DIARY

May 3, 1801

Hiram came for me today. While it is not as I would have it, I have such faith in him that I came most gladly. Hiram is out now but he will soon return and we will have our first night …

60 CAMERA PULLS BACK

as there is a sound at the door, and Mary stops writing. She hastily slips the diary into a secret drawer in desk and stands up to face the door as Hiram steps into the cabin. She runs into his arms.

MARY

Hiram! I thought you'd never come back.

HIRAM (embraces her roughly)

Miss me, gal?

MARY

So much. But now that you're here everything is—almost perfect.

>   HIRAM (scowling)

Still harpin' on that?

>   MARY (demurely)

It would make me the happiest woman in the world.

>   HIRAM (suddenly laughs and picks her up)

There'll be a circuit rider* through Hocking next month.

Maybe we'll talk about it then.

61 ANOTHER ANGLE

as Hiram carries her across cabin toward the bed. CAMERA FOLLOWS

until they reach the bed and then

>   FADES OUT

---

* A circuit rider was a traveling clergyman of that time. (All footnotes were added
by the editor.)

ONE

"Do you, Milo, take this woman, to have and to hold, in sickness and health, till death do you part?"

"I do," I said.

"Do you, Greta, take this man ..."

There was a mumbling monotone to his voice, like a bee trying to tunnel through cotton, and I let the words slip past me. I looked down at the girl who stood beside me. All of this had been planned for several months, but she looked startled just the same. She had long black hair, a figure that stopped traffic, and a face that might have been looking out of an old Egyptian coin. Her name, for another few seconds, was Greta Brooks. I had first met her two years before in East Berlin.*

I felt a little startled myself. This was a new kind of caper for me. But it had been when I met her, too. The name is Milo March. My identification card says I'm an insurance investigator. Which means that if somebody lifts your family jewels and you have them insured with one of about two dozen insurance companies, I get them back for you—it says here in small print.

That's part of the time. I work for the Inter-World Insurance Service Corporation in Denver, Colorado. Inter-World is owned by Niels Bancroft. His admiration for me stops just

---

* See *No Grave for March* by M.E. Chaber.

short of raising my salary, and whenever anybody else has a problem, he is apt to promise that I will solve it.

That was what happened two years ago. Somebody had mislaid a British diplomat, and he'd turned up in the lost-and-found department of the Communist government of East Germany. Until that moment I couldn't have sworn that Karl Marx wasn't one of the Marx brothers, but suddenly I was loaned to the State Department and was on my way to Germany, posing as a fugitive Communist. The general idea was that I was to bring the diplomat back.

I did, but the mission would have been a flop if it hadn't been for Greta. She had been temporarily taken in by the Reds, but by the time I'd arrived she'd already discovered that they were about as democratic as a hangman's noose. She wanted out. So did I. The British diplomat didn't, but we took him along with us when we went.

For two years we'd carried on a romance of sorts in the damnedest places. We'd held hands beneath the conference tables of congressional investigating committees and kissed in the corridors of the FBI. Finally she was cleared by every government agency, with the possible exception of the Department of Wildlife, and we were left to our own devices. These had led us to the present situation.

There was a silence in the room, and I had a vague recollection of the voice saying something about "man and wife." I guessed that the ceremony was over and kissed the bride. Nobody screamed, so I must have been right.

There weren't many people there for the wedding. We'd invited Niels Bancroft and a few friends. Maybe fifteen people. They crowded around us for the congratulations. As soon as that was over, we were supposed to go out to a combination breakfast and lunch, which was on Niels. After that, Greta and I would take off for a week in the mountains.

The door opened and a big, gray-haired man stepped into the room. It was Lieutenant Murray Malikoff of the Denver Police. We were friendly, but I hadn't invited him to the wedding because I knew he was on duty. I decided he must have been in the neighborhood and had taken advantage of it.

"You're just in time to kiss the bride," I said.

He grinned a little tightly as though he were tired. He went over and pecked at Greta's cheek. Then he shook my hand.

"Congratulations, Milo," he said. "I hope you have better luck with the rest of the marriage than with the beginning."

"What does that mean?" I asked.

"You're under arrest, Milo."

For a minute I thought it was a gag. "You mean the rest of my wives have caught up with me?" I asked.

Murray shook his head seriously. "This is no joke, Milo. The department has been requested to arrest you."

"By whom?"

"The Department of Justice."

The brief exchange of information had accomplished one thing. It had stopped all the conversation in the room.

"Then where's the FBI?" I asked. I still wasn't sure that it wasn't a joke. "They usually do the arresting for the Department."

He nodded. "Brown, in the local FBI office, is the one who asked me to bring you in. He knows I'm your friend and he thought that might make it easier."

"Oh, sure," I said. "I always like to be arrested by my friends. What's the charge?"

"They just want you for questioning."

I didn't know what it was about, but that didn't sound so bad. "All right," I said. "Let's go down to this Brown's office; he can ask his questions and then Greta and I can be on our way."

"It isn't quite that simple, Milo," the Lieutenant said. "I don't know what it's all about. Neither does Brown. But they want you for questioning in New York."

"New York?" I said blankly.

"We'll fight it," roared Niels Bancroft. That was my boss. He was always eager to fight over somebody else's body. "We're not going to be frightened by the FBI!"

"Share and share alike," I said bitterly. "I'll go to jail and Niels will do the yelling."

He gave me a look that said I didn't appreciate him. The look was right. I didn't.

Greta edged closer and slipped her hand into mine. "What is it, Milo?" she asked.

"I don't know, honey," I said. "Maybe the junior senator is scraping the bottom of the barrel." But nobody was in the mood for jokes, even feeble ones. "Niels is right about one thing, honey. We'll do something about it. Maybe they'll hold off their questioning for a week."

"I suggested that," the Lieutenant said. He looked unhappy. "They won't wait. I talked over the whole situation with Brown. You have two choices, Milo. You can fight going to New York if you want to. In that case, however, I'll have to take you in and hold you until a decision is made."

"That's a lovely choice," I said brightly, "but I don't think I care for it. I don't recall that there's a bridal suite in the local jail. What's the other choice?"

"I explained the whole situation to Brown," Lieutenant Malikoff said, "and he made a suggestion. If you will agree to go voluntarily to New York, I can take you straight to the airport and put you on a plane. In fact, there's one in about a half hour. It'll put you in New York in four and a half hours. Brown says that with luck you'll be through with the questioning in about an hour. You can take the next plane back and be in Denver tonight. So it will delay your honeymoon by only a few hours."

"There's only one thing I don't like about it," I said. "That phrase 'with luck.' What does it mean?"

Lieutenant Malikoff shrugged. "I don't know what they want to question you about, so I can't say. I suppose it refers to the answers you give."

"And with another kind of luck I could end up in Alcatraz, I suppose," I said.

"You know your own vulnerability better than I do," he said dryly.

I grinned. "The only thing I can think of is that I have some intention of impairing the morals of my wife. Is that illegal?"

"Some places it is," he said. "Seriously, Milo, I'm told that the questioning is a matter of routine despite the fact that there is some urgency on their part. Whatever the case is, the department does not believe that you are directly involved—only that you may be able to provide needed information."

"That's fine as far as it goes," I said. "Information on what?"

"I don't know."

"Milo," Greta said, putting her hand on my arm, "why not go voluntarily? Murray says you'll be able to be back here by night, so at the most we'll lose only the afternoon."

She was right. There was no point in being stuffy about it. If the Department of Justice wanted me, they'd get me one way or the other, so I might as well make it easy on myself. "Okay, honey," I said. "I'll do it."

"Good," the Lieutenant said. "Come on. I'll take you to the airport. There's just about enough time to make the next flight."

"You mean they'll trust me to go alone?" I asked.

"At my suggestion," he said. "Just remember that, if you get any sudden ideas about taking off into the wild blue yonder."

"With Greta here as a hostage? Not a chance. Where do I have to go when I reach New York—the Justice Department?"

He shook his head. "Immigration and Naturalization Service at Seventy Columbus Circle."

"Immigration?" I said. "What the hell can I tell them about immigration?"

"Maybe," Greta said hesitatingly, "it has to do with your bringing me back from Germany."

"Couldn't be," I said. "You were a citizen."

"Save it for later," Malikoff said. "We don't have much time."

So I kissed Greta, listened patiently to a number of funny fellows who offered to take care of the bride, and went down to the street with Lieutenant Malikoff. We got into the police car and got under way.

"A fine thing," I grumbled. "If anybody asks me where we spent our honeymoon, I'll have to say that she went to the mountains and I went to New York City."

He grunted something.

"Then," I said, "if anybody wants to know why, I suppose I can always say that I'd been to the mountains." He opened the siren and that was his only answer. I didn't blame him. It didn't deserve any more than that.

With the help of the siren we went through Denver without stopping. There were still three minutes before flight time when we arrived at the airport. I'd been wondering if I'd be able to get a seat, but I discovered that the FBI had taken care of that. They'd made a reservation.

"Okay, Murray," I said. "I'm off in my own custody. Who do I see when I get there?"

"Gardner. He's expecting you. And don't worry about getting back tonight, Milo. The Bureau will also see to it that you have a reservation on the return flight."

"They're so good to me," I said dryly. I bought a mystery novel at the newsstand—it wasn't exactly what I'd been looking forward to, but it would have to do—and climbed aboard the plane. Two minutes later we took off.

It was a four-and-a-half-hour flight, and the mystery novel took care of no more than one fourth of it. After that I chain-smoked and wondered what the hell the Immigration Service could want with me. I'd done a lot of things in my life, but so far as I could remember, I'd never smuggled anyone in or out of the country.

It was the middle of the afternoon when we sat down on

LaGuardia Field. If I'd been patting myself on the back over the fact that they'd let me come alone, I soon got over it. There was a Bureau man waiting there for me. He drove me into the city and delivered me at the office on Columbus Circle.

Mr. Gardner saw me right away. He looked so much less official than the Bureau man who had just escorted me that I immediately felt more relaxed. He talked to me pleasantly about my flight for two or three minutes until a secretary came in with a folder. She placed it on the desk and walked out. There was just enough jiggle to her hips to remind me that I was supposed to be on my honeymoon instead of sitting in a New York office.

By the time I got my gaze back to Mr. Gardner he had opened the folder and was looking more official. I reluctantly forgot about hips and honeymoons.

"Mr. March," he said, "I believe that you made a trip to Spain within the last year.* Is that correct?"

"Yes."

"For what purpose?"

"To recover a rather valuable diamond." I wondered what he was after. I'd probably broken a few Spanish laws while I was there, but I hadn't broken any American ones.

"I believe you also brought back the man who had stolen the diamond?"

"That's right," I said. "But he was an American citizen and he agreed to come voluntarily with me."

He nodded. "So I understand. Now, Mr. March, while you

---

* See *The Man Inside* by M.E. Chaber.

were about the business of apprehending him in Spain, did you use any Spanish nationals to help you with the search?"

I started to say that I hadn't, then realized that wasn't strictly true. "Yes. I did have a boy shadow the man for a number of days."

He glanced at the folder. "Was that one Ernesto Pujol?"

"Yes." I hitched my chair a little closer to his desk. "Now, if you don't mind, I'd like to know what this is all about. So far, no one has told me anything."

He put the folder down on the desk and placed the tips of his fingers together. He peered at me over the tops of them. "Yesterday," he said, "a stowaway was discovered on one of the big liners after it had docked. He is a Spanish national. He has given his name as Ernesto Pujol and has informed us, through interpreters, that he came here because you told him to."

I grinned. I remembered Ernesto all right, and that sounded just like him. He was a real tough little Spanish kid who had lived on the streets from the time he could walk. He'd been ten years old when I met him and he was then the chief support for his mother and father and nine brothers and sisters and an aunt. Although he was ten, he was no larger than a boy of seven or eight. I could still remember the way he'd looked when I first saw him. His clothes were clean but ragged, fitting him in a way that suggested they'd been handed down from generation to generation. The olive skin of his face was drawn tightly over the cheekbones, making his eyes look like two black coals. The expression in his eyes had been that of a cynical old man. Life didn't have many surprises for Ernesto. I'd liked him right at the start. I had used him to help me. Ernesto had not only liked the money, for it was more than he could earn shining shoes, but he had thought of us as a couple of Humphrey Bogarts.

"Well, Mr. March?"

"Sorry," I said. "I was just remembering Ernesto. He was quite a boy. I suspect stowing away on a liner would be easy for him."

"Very possibly. But what I wanted to know was if you suggested that he do it."

"Not in the way you're suggesting," I said, "but I remember something that may have put the idea in Ernesto's head. When I was leaving Spain I remember that he said that someday he would come to America and we would be partners again. Half-jokingly I told him sure."

"That was all, Mr. March?"

"That was all. Ernesto was always pretty good at thinking up his own ideas."

"Very well, Mr. March. We suspected that the boy was lying, but we wanted to make sure. I think that's all we need from you."

"You think so, do you?" I asked. I was getting annoyed. "You brought me all the way from Denver, interrupting my honeymoon, just to ask me that one question. Then you're through with me and the kid's a liar. Is that the way it is?"

"More or less correct," he said coldly.

"And what happens to Ernesto?" I asked.

"He'll be kept in custody on Ellis Island until we can return him to Spain."

I had a flash vision of Ernesto's face as he'd get the news. I don't know whether it was that, knowing that he would feel that I'd let him down, or the feeling that Ernesto and I were both being misused, but whatever the reason I was getting angrier all the time.

"The hell you will," I said. "I'll do something about it. I'll adopt him—or something."

He gave me a bureaucratic smile. "You are privileged to try, Mr. March," he said, "but I feel it only proper to warn you that it may not be that easy. Undoubtedly the child has parents in Spain, and if not, then I imagine the Spanish government will have something to say about the matter."

"And Franco to you too," I snapped.* I got up and marched out of the office without waiting to hear any more from him. Ernesto's cause had become mine.

The first thing I did was put in a call to Greta. I told her what it was about and the way I was feeling. She did what I knew she would. She insisted that I do everything I could to adopt Ernesto and bring him back with me. That was my girl.

After that I shifted into high gear. I went up to one insur-

---

* Milo's retort appears to be simply a random jab at the Fascist dictator Francisco Franco, who ruled Spain 1939–1975. But the immigrant official's belief that the Spanish government would object to Ernesto's adoption is contradictory to a huge scandal that took place in Spain during the Franco era: the abduction of hundreds of thousands of babies from their mothers, primarily as a means of ridding Spain of "undesirables" such as leftists and poor people who were considered economic liabilities. Those babies were then allegedly sold to other couples. (One can't help thinking of Crossen's 1940 Green Lama pulp story "Babies for Sale.") But it seems impossible that Crossen could have known about the Spanish baby-stealing even in 1954 when *As Old as Cain* was published. Rumors about this monstrous practice abounded, but it took decades before it was prosecuted. It's ironic that Milo ends up paying a price for Ernesto. Another irony is that the "McCarran Subversive Activities Act" of 1950, mentioned by Milo later on, was the American way of keeping out undesirable left-wingers.

ance company that was still grateful for the last job I'd done. They loaned me one of their lawyers, and the lawyer was the pal of a judge. After that the real business started. We dragged the Spanish consul away from an early cocktail party. We put in a phone call to Madrid. Then we waited around until our call was returned. After a lot of talk that ran up a fancy overseas phone bill, it turned out that Señor and Señora Pujol didn't mind if their Ernesto was adopted by a wealthy *americano,* although they did think they ought to have a little consolation present. I agreed to send them a hundred dollars.

The Spanish consul also talked to Madrid at my expense and then gave his blessing to the matter. After that we went back to the judge. There was some more red tape and finally the judge gave me a paper which put Ernesto in my custody until the adoption could go through.

Armed with the paper, I went over to Ellis Island. An official examined the paper as if he expected to find a refugee under the typed letters, and finally led me into a little room. I waited there. About twenty minutes later the door opened and Ernesto came in.

He looked pretty much as he had when I'd last seen him a year before. He might have grown a little, but certainly not much. His clothes still hung on him in a way that made him look like a junior Don Quixote. A big grin split his thin face as he saw me.

"Ernesto," I said, *"Qué aires te traen por aquí?"*

His grin became even wider. *"Oye, tú,"* he exclaimed happily. "Don Milo, I knew that you would come with the speed of the wind if these mules only notified you that I had arrived."

"It was more like a gentle breeze," I said dryly. "Tell me, Ernesto, what caused you to make this trip?"

"But it was agreed, Don Milo," he said in surprise. "When you were leaving Madrid, it was said that I would one day come to America and we would work together again."

"So we did," I said. I was beginning to realize I'd been trapped by my own emotions, but I couldn't exactly say I was sorry. There was something so appealing about Ernesto, and I could guess how much this meant to him. "But who is taking care of all the little Pujoles?"

"Antonio and Andrés have become bootblacks on the Puerto del Sol. The money you so kindly gave me in Madrid has served to buy a small shop for my Tía Ana. They are all well and sent me off with good wishes."

"Well, that seems to settle that. Let's go, Ernesto."

"*Claro que sí.*"

"*Aguarda un momento,* Ernesto," I said. "What about your luggage?"

"I am wearing it," he said simply.

"Let's go, then." I led the way out of there. The atmosphere of Ellis Island had always depressed me, and I was probably happier to get out of there than he was.

"This is a very mountain of a city," he exclaimed as we reached Manhattan. "Do you live in one of these palaces, Don Milo?"

"Hardly," I said. "My palace is an apartment in Denver, several hundred miles from here."

"*No me diga!*" he exclaimed. "Where are we going now, Don Milo?"

"To telephone your new mother."

"My mother? In Madrid?"

"In Denver. You see, Ernesto, in order to make it possible for you to stay in America, I have arranged to adopt you. As it happens, I just got married today, so you have a new mother."

"But, Don Milo," he said in an aggrieved tone, "I thought I was coming to work and live with you, man to man."

"There are laws, Ernesto," I tried to explain. "This was the only way you could stay in America."

"But women … ," he said scornfully.

"The tone will change in time," I said dryly. "As for working, Ernesto, in America you will have to go to school."

"School is for girls, not men."

"In America it is for all," I said firmly. "You will have to go to school, Ernesto."

"All day?"

"Part of the day."

"They will teach me the English?"

"Yes."

"They will teach me to be like Don Humphrey Bogart?"

"That part I can't guarantee."

"And when I am not in school, I will be able to work with you as partners?"

"I guess so," I said, wondering what I was letting myself in for.

"Very well," he said with dignity, "I will stay, then. We will go talk to the new mother."

We went across town until we found a building where there were phone booths and a switchboard for long-distance calls. I put in a call to Inter-World. Greta was still there, waiting for me.

"Hi, honey," I said when she came on the phone. "I finally got him."

"Wonderful," she said. "Should—should I speak to him?"

"It would be difficult. He doesn't speak much English. Besides, he hates women."

"Oh, dear."

"Don't worry. He'll change his mind when he sees you. Now, look, honey, I'm sorry this took up so much time, but we still ought to be able to get to Denver by about eleven-thirty. Then we'll get somebody to look after Ernesto and we'll finally get started on our honeymoon. Love me?"

"I do love you, Milo," she said. She sounded like she meant it, but she still didn't sound as delighted over the fact that I was coming back as I had expected.

"Is there something wrong, honey?" I asked.

"Just a minute, Milo," she said. "Mr. Bancroft wants to talk to you. Take care of yourself, darling."

I should have caught on right then, but I didn't.

"Milo." Niels Bancroft's voice boomed through the telephone into my ear. "You got the boy all right?"

"Yeah," I said, "but can't you wait until I get back to get the details? I have to catch a plane."

"I know," he said. "That's why I had to talk to you—so you'll know which plane to take."

"I know which one to take," I said sourly. "The next flight to Denver."

"There's been a slight change in plans," he said with the kind of false gentleness he always assumes when he's trying to put something over. "You're taking a plane to Columbus, Ohio, then going by train or rented car to Athens, Ohio. No reason why you can't take the boy with you, and then he can come back here with you. It'll give him a chance to see some of the country."

"Just wait a minute," I said. "Have you flipped your lid? I just got married today. I'm coming back to Denver, and Greta and I are going on a one-week honeymoon. Remember?"

"My dear Milo, of course I remember. Didn't I give the bride away? That's why I'm brokenhearted about this change of plans."

"I haven't made any change of plans. I'm coming back to Denver."

"Of course you are. But first you're going to Athens, Ohio. It's a rush job for Great Northern. John Franklin is waiting in their New York office to give you the details. He'll give you some expense money, too. It'll take you twenty-four hours at the most."

"No," I said firmly.

"It's not a big job," he said, "but it is a rush and Great Northern won't have anybody but you do it."

"No," I said again. "I'm coming straight home."

His voice lost its velvet glove. "If you don't do this job, you won't have a job when you get back here. That will be a fine way to start out with a new wife and a new son."

I told him what I thought he ought to do with his job. "I can always get a job with one of the insurance companies," I added.

"Not," he said with deadly sweetness, "if Great Northern and Inter-World both pass around the word that you're unreliable."

He was right. He knew it and I knew it. As usual, he had me right over a barrel.

"You're just not thinking, boy," he said. His voice was friendly again. "There's nothing to it. This is just a routine job that won't take you more than twenty-four hours. You should be back here by tomorrow night and ready to start that honeymoon. Maybe you can even take two weeks instead of one."

I knew when I was licked, but I wasn't going to admit it out loud. I put the receiver back on the hook and stepped out of the booth. Then I expressed a few thoughts I had about Niels Bancroft.

"Before God, Don Milo," Ernesto said admiringly, "this English of yours is a most powerful language."

"At times," I admitted, grinning. "I was indulging in a little swearing, Ernesto, and I have discovered that such words are powerful in any language."

"It is the woman, Don Milo?"

"It is not the woman, Ernesto," I said. "It is the man for whom I work. He is a blackmailing son of a woman of ill repute."

"Es un mal bicho?"

"*Cierto,*" I said. "He is most certainly a bad egg."

"You are my friend, Don Milo," he said. "You would like me to take care of this *hombre?*" From the midst of his ragged clothes, he produced a switchblade knife.

"No," I said hurriedly. "And, Ernesto, there is a law here

against carrying such knives. You'd better give it to me." I held out my hand.

"*Es un país absurdo,*" he grumbled, but he handed over the knife.

I closed the blade and put the knife in my pocket. "Let's go, Ernesto."

"Where, Don Milo? To this Denver?"

"Not yet," I said sourly. "We have to do some work first. I seem to be in the position of having acquired a wife and a family without benefit of more than a wedding ceremony and one kiss."

TWO

The New York offices of the Great Northern Insurance Company were empty when we arrived, but John Franklin was still there. He was a big man, about forty-five years of age. His tailoring and barbering were those of a high-salaried executive, but he still looked like a cop. Which was what he had been before he went to Great Northern to head up their investigation department.

"Milo, how are you?" he said warmly, shaking my hand. His gaze dropped to Ernesto. "Who's this? A junior G-man?"

"This is Ernesto," I said. I switched to Spanish. "Ernesto, this is my friend Don John Franklin."

"Mucho gusto, Señor," Ernesto said.

"Ernesto speaks no English," I explained to Franklin. "He's my son." I felt a little foolish making the statement, but since I was adopting him it was true.

John Franklin's eyebrows lifted. "I didn't know you were married."

"I just got married this morning," I said shortly. "I'm supposed to be on my honeymoon right now instead of chasing off someplace for you."

"And you've already got a son?" he said. He threw back his head and laughed. "No wonder the boy can't speak English. You've rushed things so much, it's already a miracle."

"Very funny," I said. "You want to go ahead making up funny cracks about my nonexistent married life or do you want to tell me about this crummy case?"

Still chuckling, he led the way into his office. He found a picture magazine for Ernesto to look at and turned his attention back to me.

"Crescent Pictures, out in Hollywood," he said, "is going to make a historical about Southern Ohio. They're going to shoot it on location, and a number of their people are there now preparing for it. I understand the picture will be built around an actual person who lived in the vicinity of Athens at the beginning of the eighteenth century. Descendants of this man are still living there, and they have in their possession a number of antiques and other objects belonging to him. These have been loaned to the picture company, which in turn is insuring them for one million dollars.* That's a lot of money."

"A lot of cabbage," I admitted. "But what does it have to do with me?"

"We've done a lot of business with Crescent," he went on, "so we have already issued the coverage they requested, subject to appraisal and investigation. The appraiser is already out there. As I understand it, the picture company has temporarily placed all the objects in a makeshift museum, which is open to the public. We want you to go down and check the people involved and the security arrangements that have been made."

"That's all?"

"That's all."

---

* More like ten million in today's dollars.

I took a deep breath and tried to keep my voice normal. "But why the hell me? You must have dozens of investigators who can make a routine job like that. Why not use them?"

"I'm sorry, Milo," he said, "but a million-dollar policy is a big one. The Board of Directors decided that on a case involving such a large sum they would prefer having you handle it. When I spoke to Niels, he said you'd be happy to undertake it. I didn't know anything about your getting married."

"Just make sure," I said grimly, "that your company doesn't issue any life insurance to Niels Bancroft. He's going to be a poor risk for the next few days. Anything else?"

"That's about it. A Mr. Lionel Moore is there appraising the objects. The only representative of the picture company, with whom you can confer on the scene, is the director of the picture, Laslo Kryle. Both gentlemen are staying at the Hocking Hotel. That's it. You can start anytime you like. Here's some expense money for you."

"How much?"

"Five hundred. That ought to be enough if you don't start buying packages of Cadillacs. If there's any left over, use it to buy yourself a wedding present."

"I'll use it to buy back my introduction to Niels Bancroft," I said. I switched languages again. "Time to go, Ernesto. Say good-bye to the nice man."

"*Adiós, anciano,*" he said. The *anciano* was a piece of impertinence, but since Franklin didn't understand Spanish, I let it pass. Ernesto and I left.

The first thing we did was hunt around until we finally found a store that was still open where we could get some new clothes for Ernesto. I bought him enough to last him until we got to Denver, included some extra linen for myself, and we went out. Ernesto was walking on air, stopping to gaze at his new finery in every store window.

A check with the airport revealed that it would be the middle of the night when we reached Columbus, Ohio. It would mean little sleep and we wouldn't reach Athens until early in the morning. I did some more checking and found we just had time to take a plane to Washington and catch the train for Athens. That would get us there at five-thirty in the morning, which was a little too early but would give us a chance to get some sleep.

We did it that way. We made the train with about one minute to spare. The New York office of the Baltimore and Ohio had reserved a bedroom, so Ernesto and I tumbled in and went to sleep.

The porter awakened us at five in the morning. It was a struggle, but I made it. At five-thirty we got out of the train in front of a small depot. A sign on the end of the building confirmed that this was Athens. The streets were deserted, not even a taxi in sight. I expressed a few more private opinions of Niels Bancroft.

Finally we found a little all-night coffee joint across the street. It was too early for me to have more than coffee, but Ernesto put away a man-sized breakfast.

"Where's the Hocking Hotel?" I asked the man behind the counter while Ernesto was polishing off his second glass of milk.

The man stopped shining the coffee urn and looked at me. "Stranger in town?" he asked.

It was too early in the morning. "No," I said. "I always get up this early in the morning and ask where the Hocking Hotel is."

He looked at me without even a suggestion of a smile. "Don't remember seeing you around before. Besides, if you lived here you'd know where the hotel is."

I took a deep breath and tried again. "Okay," I said. "I'm a stranger in town. I just got off the train. I want to know how to find the Hocking Hotel."

"Why didn't you say so in the first place?" he asked. "You just go up this street here until you get to Court Street. Turn left and go up past the courthouse and you'll see the hotel right past it."

"What about getting a taxi?" I asked.

"Reckon you'll have to walk. No taxis around this time of morning."

"Great," I said. I didn't think there was going to be any great romance between Athens and me. "Ready, Ernesto?"

"*Listo,*" he said cheerfully.

The counterman looked interested as we slid off the stools. "Foreigners?" he asked.

"No," I said shortly. "We just talk that way early in the morning. It takes two or three hours for us to warm up to English. How much do we owe you?"

"Dollar thirty," he said. He sounded annoyed. I couldn't think why.

I tossed the money on the counter, and Ernesto and I walked up the street. There were a couple of milk trucks out, but that was all. Everyone else was asleep. Or maybe the town always looked like that. I knew I wasn't being fair, but I wasn't in any mood for it.

Ernesto chattered about everything he saw as we walked along. I grunted whenever his voice stopped, but that seemed to satisfy him. We reached Court Street and turned left. It seemed to be the main street. We walked a couple of blocks before we found the hotel.

An elderly man was dozing behind the desk. A kid was doing the same in a chair in the lobby.

I walked up to the desk and slapped my hand down on it. The old man opened his eyes and looked at me, waiting.

"We want two rooms, adjoining," I said.

"Guess we can fix you up." He swung the register around, his gaze taking in the package I carried. "No luggage?"

"No luggage, but we'll be happy to pay in advance. We'll probably check out sometime tonight."

Ernesto had been busily examining the lobby. *"Paramos aquí?"* he asked.

"We're stopping here," I admitted.

"It is truly a palace," he said admiringly. "A man could live here like a king."

"A king might have a different idea about it," I murmured.

The clerk had been looking at us as we spoke. "What language is that?" he asked.

"Spanish."

"That so? Don't get many Spaniards around this way." He glanced at the register where I had written *Milo March and son.* "Your wife didn't come with you this trip, eh?"

"She's on her honeymoon." I grinned at the expression on

his face and continued. "You have a Lionel Moore and a Laslo Kryle staying here?"

He nodded. "Yes, sir."

"Do you know what time they're usually up?"

"Pretty late. We got five of them movie people here, and they go to bed later and get up later than anybody I ever knew. I guess them Hollywood people are pretty wild."

"The wildest," I agreed. "When either Mr. Moore or Mr. Kryle gets up, will you see that they are told that Mr. March, of the Great Northern Insurance Company, is here and waiting for them to get in touch with him?"

"Sure will."

"I don't suppose," I said, knowing damn well what the answer would be, "that it's possible to get a drink this early in the morning?"

He stared at me doubtfully, then made an effort to give me the benefit of doubt. "Water?"

"Whiskey," I amended cheerfully.

His mouth became a thin line. "No," he said. Just the way he said it made me even dryer.

So I paid him and he awakened the bellboy, who took us upstairs to the rooms. As soon as he was gone, I told Ernesto he could take either room he wanted and go back to sleep if he wanted to.

"You mean, Don Milo," he said, "that one of these huge rooms is just for me?"

"Just for you."

"Truly you must be a millionaire," he said. His eyes were wide with wonder.

"I'm a few dollars away from it," I said dryly.

Ernesto wasn't listening. He ran into the bathroom and turned all the faucets, one by one. He looked in the medicine chest back of the mirror. He flushed the toilet. He ran back into the bedroom, opening dresser drawers, then jumped on the bed and started bouncing.

"*Estupendo!*" he exclaimed. "*Ahora rueda el dinero más que nunca! Pues mira, chico, déjate de rodeos y contesta claramente.*"

"No," I said, "the money is not rolling in. In America many people stay at hotels like this, often even better. I give it to you straight, *chico.*"

"Truly?"

"Truly," I said. "Now you amuse yourself for a while. I can't talk to anybody and I can't get a drink, so I'm going into the next room and see if I can sleep some more. Okay?"

"*Bueno,*" he said. "I shall be as quiet as the winds from the Guadarrama."

I went into the next room and stretched out on the bed. I wanted to phone Greta, but I knew she'd probably be asleep. Thinking about her, I finally dozed off.

The sharp ringing of the phone knifed through my sleep and brought me up out of the bed. I looked at my watch. It was ten o'clock. I picked up the receiver.

"Yeah?" I said.

"Mr. March?"

"Yeah."

"This is Lionel Moore. What time did you get in?"

"At five-thirty, God help me."

He groaned in sympathy. "I'm down in the dining room with the Crescent people having breakfast. Why not join us?"

"Be right down," I said. I pressed down the bar on the phone cradle, waited a minute, and released it. When the operator came on, I gave her the number of the phone in my apartment in Denver. I knew that Greta would have stayed there the night before. I listened to operators being polite to each other across the country, then finally she was on the phone.

I suppose we said all the same things that brides and bride-grooms have been saying for years, but they didn't sound as if they'd been said before. I assured her that I'd be back sometime that night and reluctantly hung up. I went into the next room. Ernesto was half out of the window, taking in the sights.

"It is a quiet pueblo," he said.

"I can imagine," I told him.

"Is it that perhaps they enjoy the siesta in the morning?"

"Morning, afternoon, and night," I said. "I'm going down to the dining room to see some people. Want to come along?"

"The dining room?"

"Yeah, you can have something," I said dryly.

"Muy bien," he said, his eyes lighting up.

"In English, the word is *okay,*" I said. "You might as well start learning it now."

"Okay," he said. He looked at me eagerly. "I will learn the English good, Don Milo."

"Well, you've got a one-word start. Let's go."

We went downstairs and into the dining room. There was

no difficulty in spotting the ones we were looking for; they were the only people in the dining room. There were four men and two women sitting at one large table. I could have spotted them just as easily if the room had been full of natives. They managed to make that one spot in the Hocking Hotel look like the Brown Derby.* Two of them were easily recognized. One was a well-stacked blond beauty, Niki Holden. Not much of an actress, but the way she was built she didn't have to act. The other was her male counterpart, Gilbert Ireland. Six foot three, with wide shoulders and a handsome profile that had half the women in America panting. I didn't recognize the others, but they all looked Hollywood except for one man. He was wearing coat and pants that matched, so he was probably the one the insurance company had sent out to appraise the stuff.

I was right. The one wearing the business suit stood up and advanced to meet me.

"Milo March?" he said.

"Right," I said. "You must be Lionel Moore. You're the only one who doesn't look like a refugee from Mike Romanoff's."** I said it low enough so the others couldn't hear, and he grinned as we shook hands.

"Glad to know you, March," he said. He glanced down at Ernesto. "A local fan?"

"My son," I said. I decided to avoid any more confusion on the subject. "Actually, I'm in the process of adopting him. He has just arrived from Spain." I switched to Spanish and introduced Moore to Ernesto.

---

* A famous Hollywood restaurant of the 1930s and '40s.
** Mike Romanoff was a self-styled "Russian prince" whose Beverly Hills restaurant, Romanoff's, was frequented by celebrities in the 1940s and '50s.

"Cómo le va," Ernesto said.

"Hi," Moore said. He reached out and shook hands gravely with Ernesto. "Come on over and meet the refugees."

"I can hardly wait," I said dryly. "When do we go look at the million bucks?"

We were approaching the table and he lowered his voice. "As soon as we're through breakfast, you'll probably get the guided tour."

We reached the table and everybody looked up.

"This is Mr. Milo March, from the insurance company," Lionel Moore said. "Milo, this is Miss Niki Holden."

The blond star was looking me over in a way that made me feel like I'd wandered into a ladies' Turkish bath. "A new man," she said. You could hear the rustle of bedsheets in her voice. "Just my type, too."

"Who isn't?" murmured Gilbert Ireland.

"You aren't, darling," she answered. There was a honed edge to her voice. "I like *men.*"

"And this," Moore said hurriedly, turning to the other girl, "is Miss Lili Robben." She was a pretty little dark-haired girl with a permanent look of amusement on her face.

"Hi," she said. "Just so you don't confuse the royalty and the peasants, I'm in the Crescent research department."

"But she'll research almost anything," Niki Holden said. The edge was still in her voice. "Our Lili has very broad interests."

"Look who's making cracks about being a broad," the researcher said flippantly.

Gilbert Ireland laughed. This was just one big happy family.

Lionel Moore was obviously embarrassed as he tried to ignore the side remarks. "This is Mr. Gilbert Ireland," he said, turning to the actor.

"How are you, March?" Ireland said casually. He wasn't looking at me, but was still giving me the benefit of the profile. I noticed he was the only one not eating breakfast. He had a cup of coffee and a glass of liquor in front of him. The glass was obviously getting more action than the cup.

"Mr. Laslo Kryle," Moore was saying. I recognized the name. He was one of Hollywood's more famous directors. He was a big man with close-cropped black hair. He wore a sport jacket that made him look like a caricature of a Hollywood character.

"Hello," he grunted briefly. He had a reputation for deliberately mangling the English language for laughs, but it was apparently too early in the morning or he had decided not to waste any wit on a mere insurance investigator. It was all right with me; I didn't feel like yakking it up.

"And Mr. Curtis Hoyt," Moore said. "He's the scriptwriter," he added as though it were meant to explain something.

Hoyt was young and sleek in a way that probably indicated he was at least a $3,000-a-week man. I wondered if the heavy-rimmed glasses he wore were a necessity or a badge of his profession.

He was the only one who offered to shake hands. "Hi, Milo," he said. "You disappoint me. You're the first private eye I've ever seen that wasn't supplied by Central Casting, and you're not wearing a trenchcoat. Wha' hoppen?"

"Sorry," I said, "but I just sent it out to have a new mink lining put in it."

He grinned. "Careful, shamus; you carry on like that and you're liable to lose your drinking-and-wenching license."

"Well," I said, "I can always get a club and change my name to Mike Hammerless."

"Not good, but fast," he said. His gaze shifted to Ernesto. "Who's the short stuff?"

"My assistant in charge of small cases," I said.

"Better and better. Hire a couple of writers to polish the lines and people might start believing you're a private eye."

"Thanks," I said dryly. "Actually, this is my adopted son, Ernesto Pujol. He's just over from Spain and doesn't understand any English, so your gags will be wasted on him." I switched to Spanish. "Ernesto, I want you to meet Señorita Niki Holden. She is a famous cinema star."

"I've seen her," he said scornfully. He looked her over, his eyes as cynical as those of an old man. "She acts only with the swinging of her hips. There are girls on the street who can do it better."

An actress may not understand a language, but she always knows when she's being talked about. Niki Holden was no exception. "What did he say about my acting?" she demanded.

"That he considered it exceptional," I said promptly. "He says that it is considered a great art in his country."

It was enough to make her waste a smile on him. "He's sweet," she said.

"But a little young for you, dear," Gilbert Ireland murmured.

"Señorita Lili Robben," I said indicating the researcher.

"Como le va, Señorita?" Ernesto said formally.

"Likewise—I hope," she said.

"Señor Laslo Kryle," I said, turning to the director.

"Como le va, Señor?"

The director grunted.

"The Señor Gilbert Ireland. Perhaps you have also seen him in the cinema."

"I've seen him," Ernesto said. "The only time I enjoyed it was the one time when, in a picture, the Señor Bogart punched him in the nose. That was wonderful."

"What's that about Bogart?" the actor demanded.

"He remembers seeing you in a picture with Bogart," I said carefully. "He thought your performance was wonderful."

He nodded thoughtfully. "The little bastard has better sense than I thought."

I turned to the writer. There was a smile on his face as though he were enjoying a secret joke.

"The gentleman who seems to be enjoying himself," I said, "is the Señor Curtis Hoyt."

"Como le va?" Ernesto said.

"Estoy muy bien, Ernesto. *De dónde eres?"*

So that was why he'd been grinning to himself. He'd understood what Ernesto had said about the two stars.

Ernesto grinned broadly. *"Soy madrileño,"* he said proudly.

"All right," I said, "you two can have a mutual admiration meeting later. Let's sit down."

"Come and sit by me, Ernesto," Curtis Hoyt said in Spanish, "and I'll tell you how bad these actors really are."

Ernesto grinned and went to sit by him. I sat down between

Lionel Moore and Niki Holden. The blonde's knee was suspiciously close to my chair and she didn't move it.

The waitress, a middle-aged woman, came over and managed to pry her gaze away from the profile long enough to ask me what I wanted to order.

"Qué quieres comer?" I asked Ernesto.

He looked thoughtful. *"Helados de chocolate?"* he asked.

"Sure," I said. "Bring the boy a double order of chocolate ice cream." I looked at him and remembered when I was a boy. "Make it a triple order. You can bring me some scrambled eggs and coffee and a double brandy." She frowned at the brandy, but went away without giving me any lectures on temperance.

"What a hick town," Niki Holden said, giving me the benefit of a wide-eyed look that was usually reserved for the camera close-ups. "How long are you going to stay with us, Milo?"

The pressure of her knee beneath the table was warm enough so that I thought I'd better get the record straight. "Not long," I said. "I'm going to take a look at the antiques your company is using, write up a report, and take off sometime this evening."

She pouted. I seemed to remember the expression from one of her pictures. I wondered if she reached back into her memory and pulled them out according to her need.

"Just my luck," she said lightly. "The first good-looking man to arrive in this joint and he's taking off again."

"As a matter of fact," I said, "I'm not even supposed to be working now. I was just married yesterday morning and I'm supposed to be on my honeymoon instead of here looking at the legs of some old table."

"Niki could take care of the honeymoon part," Gilbert Ireland said.

The blond star laughed with the rest of us, but I noticed that she didn't deny it. I decided I'd better try to get out of town before I had to fight for my so-called honor.

"A lot of nonsense," Laslo Kryle grumbled suddenly. "Why do you have to come shlepping down here to look at a lot of old junk? It's a waste of your time and a waste of our time."

"A million dollars' worth of junk," I reminded him.

"A million dollars," he said, dismissing it as though it were small change dropped from his pocket. "Junk is junk even if it's money. We're supposed to be making a picture, not dealing in secondhand furniture."

"I don't think we need to interfere with you," I said. "You can go ahead with your junk and I'll go ahead with my junk."

"And never the abandoned twains shall meet—if you'll excuse my baby talk," Curtis Hoyt murmured. "I probably should object to one of those junks, being the author of same, but I'll pass."

"Everything is cleared, Mr. Kryle," Lionel Moore said. "You're not using any of the objects in question yet, and it will not be necessary for any of you people to waste any time. I will take Mr. March to see the objects and no one else will be required. But, as I pointed out in my own case, the policy on these objects was issued subject to the reports of Mr. March and myself."

"You're not shooting yet, are you?" I asked.

"No," the director said. He glared around the table. "Sometimes I think we'll never shoot. Last week we had a script; this week I don't know if we have one or not."

"Don't get in a rash," Curtis Hoyt said. "I'm in the process of giving you a better script. It'll probably get you an Oscar."

"Oscars," snorted the director. "If I need a doll, I'll go out and buy one."

The waitress arrived with my order. She sniffed audibly as she set down my brandy, but maybe it only meant she liked the smell of it.

"Pleasant little fellow, our director," Hoyt said. "The truth of the matter is that this is just a preliminary jaunt to the location. We won't start shooting the picture for five or six months. In the meantime, some new material turned up and I'm doing some rewriting on the script."

"What kind of a movie is it?" I asked. I didn't really care, but it would help to make conversation—and help me to forget the blonde's knee—while I had my breakfast.

"It's a great story," the writer said modestly. "It's built around two guys who came out to the Ohio territory before 1800. One of them was Moses Hewit, and we've got some business in it about his capture by the Indians—all legit, you understand. His pal was a guy named Hiram Hanna, and he's our hero. He lived right around here from about 1797 until he died in 1807. Just to give you an idea, Ohio University got its first state charter in 1804, and Athens County was formed in 1805."

"Sounds pretty suspenseful so far," I said.

"We got plenty of that, too," he said. "Old Hiram Hanna was quite a boy. He not only fought the Indians, but anybody else who wouldn't run. He had two women—wives—so there's enough romance, too. Plenty of action."

"The insured objects," Lionel Moore put in, "originally belonged to Hiram Hanna."

"I'm thrilled," I said. "Hiram personally hand them over?"

"In a way," Hoyt said. "There are two dames living here in this town who are descended from the old boy. One from his first wife, the other from his second. They had the furniture and stuff tucked away in their attics."

"It is doubtful, from what I hear," Moore said, "that they were even aware that most of the stuff was valuable. They just thought of it as family heirlooms."

"But from my angle," Hoyt continued, "the best find came from another angle. Back in 1804 one of the first libraries was started out here in the next county. It had an official name, but most of the first books were bought with proceeds from the hides of raccoons that Hiram Hanna and others caught, so it was called the Coonskin Library. Ain't that a killer? Well, an old guy named Enoch Drake owns that library now, and we've got him and his books lined up."

"Another fantastic situation," Moore murmured. "The collection of books is worth at least a hundred thousand dollars. Mr. Drake not only seems unaware of their value, but it's doubtful if he's ever looked inside one of the books. He apparently kept them only because they were inherited from his father. Otherwise he might have thrown them out." He shuddered at the thought.

"But get this," Hoyt said with enthusiasm. "Among the books are some that were owned by Hiram Hanna, and there's a diary that was kept by Hiram's second wife. It's a honey."

"He's a dirty little peeping Tom," Niki Holden said. "He

spends all his time drooling over that poor woman's diary and making a big thing out of the fact that he's the only one who's seen it."

The writer leaned forward and stared owlishly at the blond star. The heavy-rimmed glasses gave the impression that he was looking at her through a microscope. "Niki, honey, you really ought to let me give you the name of my analyst when we get back to Hollywood," he said. His gaze shifted back to me. "We've taken over all the old stuff and put it in a house we've rented. The Crescent Museum, open to the public from nine to five. A great publicity gag. We've hired Enoch Drake to be in charge. It's probably the first job he's had in twenty years, and he's grateful. Besides, he likes me, so he won't let anyone else look at the diary until I'm through with it." He laughed. "There's some university professor who's down there every day begging to get a look at it. He's about to flip his lid because he hasn't seen anything but the cover."

"I think Niki is right," Lili Robben said. "Curtis is either a peeping Tom or has some kind of a secrecy fixation. He's always afraid somebody's going to steal every precious word he drops on the clean white paper. It probably has something to do with his early training."

"Hollywood intellectuals," said Hoyt. "They read a book by Bergler* and think they're educated."

"Bitches all," Gilbert Ireland said suddenly. I could see he was well on the way to being drunk.

Ernesto had finished his ice cream and was leaning back,

---

* Edmund Bergler was a Freudian psychoanalyst who wrote books about assorted neuroses.

his eyes following the conversation like it was a Ping-Pong ball. He couldn't understand it, but I could see by his expression that he had already decided that everyone was a little crazy. Maybe he was right at that.

"Seriously," Hoyt said to me, "the diary is giving me a lot of background and character stuff I didn't have before. I'm doing a major rewrite, and when I'm through this is going to be one of the most terrific movies to ever come out of Hollywood."

"What's the name of this little epic?" I asked him.

"West to the Hocking."

"Going to shoot it here?"

"That's why we're here," he said. "The two stars are supposed to"—he hesitated and looked at Gilbert Ireland, then grinned— "soak up atmosphere and all that. Laslo is going to work out production details, and our little Lili will make notes for everybody. And I'm rewriting the script."

"I'd think the place looks a little different now than it did in 1804," I said.

"Sure. But Crescent bought up a farm just out of town and they're going to build Athens and the university out there just the way it was in 1804. The picture will be shot there. And you know what they're going to do with it when the picture is finished?"

"Send it back to Greece," I suggested.

He gave me a brief grin. "The whole set will be given to the town of Athens and they're going to use it to celebrate the one hundred and fiftieth anniversary of the founding of Athens County. The first showing of the picture will be held at the opening of the celebration. Some publicity, huh?"

"Yeah," I said. "How long are the insured antiques involved?"

"I don't know," he said.

"I understand," Lionel Moore said, "that the articles will be loaned to Crescent Pictures until after the opening of the anniversary celebration late next year. The insurance policies will be in force until that time. They will then be returned to their owners, who are Miss Malvyna Hanna, Mrs. Captola Singer, and Mr. Enoch Drake."

"Okay," I said. I sipped at the last of my coffee. It was cold. "Let's go look at the antiques. *Vamos,* Ernesto."

"Ernesto isn't interested in antiques," Curtis Hoyt said. "Why not let him stay with me while you're wandering on tiptoe through the Chippendale?" He turned and translated what he'd said for Ernesto.

"If he wants to," I said.

Ernesto did want to, so I left it at that. *"Hasta luego,* Ernesto," I said. "Ready, Moore?"

He nodded and got to his feet. The waitress saw we were getting ready to leave and hurried over with our checks. I guess she thought we were all from Hollywood.

"I hope I'll see you again, Milo," Niki Holden said as I left the pressure of her knee.

"Maybe," I said.

Laslo Kryle, the director, had been staring gloomily at the empty plate in front of him through most of the talk. Suddenly he raised his gaze, flicking it over most of those at the table before looking at me.

"Picture business," he said, making it sound like a four-letter word. "It would be wonderful if it weren't for actors, actresses, and writers. I should've stayed a Hungarian pastry chef."

"Plenty of dough in that, eh, Laslo?" Hoyt said.

Kryle glared at the writer. "Writers. They get three thousand dollars a week and they think money grows under cabbage leaves."

"It's babies that are found under cabbage leaves," Lili Robben said solemnly. "Money grows on trees."

"They didn't find Laslo under a cabbage leaf," Niki Holden said. "It was a thorn bush."

"Bitches all," Gilbert Ireland muttered drunkenly.

The director was glaring at them as Moore and I left. We paid our checks and went out on the street.

"How do we get to this museum?" I asked.

"We could walk," he said, "but it's a little far. If we walk up this way a block, we can get a cab."

"The cab, by all means," I said. "Keeping up with the Joneses of Hollywood always wears me out." We walked up the street toward the courthouse.

"They are a little odd," Moore said. His voice held a mixture of awe and distaste. "Are they all like that?"

"Only more so," I said.

"It's strange," he said. "My wife and I have always enjoyed the pictures of Miss Holden and Mr. Ireland. It's rather startling to discover that Mr. Ireland is so addicted to alcohol and Miss Holden is—well—"

"A very good way of putting it," I said. "Has the blond darling of the giant screen been making passes at you?"

He looked uncomfortable. "She did suggest that I come to her room last night. She was rather insistent, but I explained I had to work on my report." He stared off into space. "Actually, I didn't have to work. Miss Holden is a very attractive woman, but I could never face Mrs. Moore if I had anything to do with her."

I felt sorry for him. Obviously he wanted to do a little wenching with the famous movie star but didn't dare. He'd probably spend the rest of his life thinking about the opportunity he'd missed. When he got to be about sixty, he'd start hating his wife and blaming her for making him miss it. Monogamy is a little like putting on a new pair of shoes: if it fits, it's wonderful, but if it's too tight, it's liable to be sheer hell.

"Miss Holden," I said dryly, "is the high priestess of the wound that never heals. It's a popular cult—according to Mr. Kinsey."

He looked blank for a minute while he groped in his mind for the picture. When he got it, he wasn't sure how to react. "That's pretty good," he said lamely.

We rounded the corner and came on a couple of cabs. We climbed into one, and a driver came ambling over.

"Want to go somewhere?" he asked.

"That was the general idea," I said.

"Where?"

Moore gave him an address on Lancaster Street. The driver got in and started the car.

"That the house them movie people took over?" he asked.

"Yes."

"You with them?"

"Not exactly," I said. "We have some business with them and that's all."

"Some chick," he said, "that blond movie star. I wouldn't mind getting next to that."

"I'll tell her," I said. "And if there's any other little thing we can do for you, why don't you drop in this evening for a social chat?"

He peered at me in the rearview mirror and finally got the idea. He muttered to himself, but shut up.

"You appraised the stuff yet?" I asked Moore.

He nodded. "I finished last night. I stayed over for your visit, but I'll be leaving this afternoon."

"How's it check out?"

"It's worth a million, all right," he said. "It's pretty hard to pin down the exact value of antiques—depends a lot on the market—but if they weren't in any hurry they could get at least that much in the world market."

"People will buy the damnedest things," I said. "Know anything about the guard setup?"

"A little. The man they hired to look after the exhibition, this Enoch Drake, lives in the house. Then Crescent has also hired a guard, a local man who's been made a special police-man. In addition to this, I understand that the local police send a man around past the house every hour or so."

"Doesn't sound like much for a million bucks."

"I don't think this is a town that runs much to crime."

"Probably not," I said. "But things may change once they start releasing the information. Also, if it's open to the public, word can spread. A lot of guys will travel a long way for a million dollars."

He shrugged. "I suppose so. But that's your problem."

"Yeah," I said sourly.

It was a short drive and we were soon there. It was an old, two-story brick house. Across the front there was a big sign reading:

THE CRESCENT PICTURES MUSEUM
Open to the Public, 9 to 5

We paid off the cab and went in. The first room was empty except for a lot of furniture. I guessed that this was part of the antiques, but it just looked old to me. There was no one in sight.

"Mr. Drake," Moore called.

A man popped in through one of the doors. He looked to be about forty-five, with a weather-beaten face from which faded blue eyes stared. He was wearing blue denim pants and shirt, with the butt of a gun sticking from the pocket of his pants. A prominent Adam's apple bobbed above the collar of his shirt.

"Didn't expect you back, Mr. Moore," he said. "Something wrong?"

"Nothing wrong," Moore said. "This is Mr. March from the insurance company."

"Howdy," he said, leaning forward to peer at me. The odor of whiskey brushed across my face.

"Mr. March," Moore went on, "is here to look over the security measures. Mind if I show him around?"

"Go right ahead. Fred's around somewhere, too. Reckon nobody'll get much of a chance to grab anything, what between Fred and my little friend here." He patted the gun butt protruding from his pocket and laughed. It sounded like a chicken cackling.

"Good. I'll show Mr. March around. You just go ahead with whatever you were doing."

"Wasn't doing anything but puttering."

"No customers, eh?"

"Nope. That university professor is here again, but that's all. I reckon everybody else's had enough of looking at old furniture." He grinned, his Adam's apple bobbing, and left.

"So that's the old family retainer," I said. I looked around the room. "The whole house filled with these things?"

"Not quite. There are four or five rooms filled with furniture and one room with books and smaller items. Unless you want to, it won't be necessary to look at every piece. The security arrangements regarding the other rooms of furniture are, I believe, identical with this room. You'd probably better check with the special policeman, but it is my understanding that there are burglar alarms in each room. These are not connected during the day. The other room, which contains the books and smaller items, has additional arrangements."

"Okay," I said. "Lead on."

"You probably wouldn't know," he said, his voice taking on the tones of a lecturer, "but these items in this room are pretty valuable. This sideboard, for example"—he put his hand on an old, scarred sideboard—"was made in 1788 by Jesse Grant of Bourbon County, Kentucky."

I wasn't impressed. "There is another item originating in Bourbon County which appeals to me more."

He gave me a weak smile. "Now, this desk. There's a secret drawer here somewhere, but I don't know how it works. It was made in 1797 by Jesse West of Clark County, Kentucky. The pillar-and-scroll mantel clock on it was made about 1800 by Eli Terry of Plymouth, Connecticut. Very rare."

"It still can't do any more than give you the time," I said.

"I suppose that is one attitude." He sounded almost as shocked as if I'd questioned his wife's chastity. "These chairs and this table were made in 1799 by John Goodman of Fayette County, Kentucky. Incidentally, in the next room, under glass, we have a copy of the *Kentucky Gazette,* published in 1799, advertising them for sale. Over here we have a weaving loom made in 1777 by William Poage of Vermont."

"Fascinating," I murmured.

"I can see how thrilled you are," he said dryly. "So I won't take you through the other rooms, but they are filled with furniture made by these men and by Thomas Affleck of Philadelphia, Thomas Tufft of Philadelphia, and Nicholas Disbrowe of Hartford, Connecticut. Shall we go along to the next room?"

"By all means," I said promptly.

We walked across the room and went through the door. We were in a room that looked as if it might have once been a large dining room. Along one wall there was a glass-enclosed bookcase with books in it. Around the room there were a number of flat cases on pedestals with glass over them.

A man stood by one of the cases. He was a big man, wearing rumpled tweeds, with a great shock of white hair. He must have been in his late fifties, but his face looked much younger. He was talking to Enoch Drake, who was grinning up at him.

"… no reason," he was saying, "why you can't let me look at the diary as long as I don't remove it from the premises. It's imperative that I see it."

The caretaker shook his head. "I told you I can't, Professor. Of course, if I'd knowed you wanted to see it before them movie people came, I'd have been glad to show it to you. But I've lent it to them and they don't want nobody snooping through it."

"But their confounded movie can't be more important than my book."

"Can't help it, Professor."

"If you could only tell me something of what's in it, then I could judge whether it's important to me or not."

"Can't," the caretaker said. "Never read anything in it. Figured it didn't make much difference what some woman wrote a hundred and fifty years ago. Now, you just relax, Professor, and when them movie people are through with it, I'll let you look at it as long as you want to."

"But that'll be next year … ," the older man began, but he stopped when Enoch Drake walked out of the room. He turned back and saw us. He looked blank for a moment, then recognition came to his face.

"It's—Mr. Moore, isn't it?" he asked. "From the insurance company, I believe?"

"Yes," Moore said. "This is Mr. March, also from the insurance company. Milo, this is Dr. Thurman Rheames. He's in the history department at Ohio University."

We shook hands.

"Still trying to get a peek at the diary, eh, Dr. Rheames?" Moore asked.

"Yes. It's very annoying. I've been working on a history of Athens County and it's about ready to go to the press. There very well may be events mentioned in the diary of Mrs. Hanna which will necessitate changes in my book. But I cannot see it, due to the whim of some motion picture scriptwriter."

"Too bad you didn't know about it before they came along," I said.

He shrugged. "I'm accustomed to that, sir. Many of the people around here have veritable treasures of Americana lying around in their attics, unnoticed. In fact, I've come across a few things quite by accident. I don't suppose either of you gentlemen could intercede with the picture people to let me see it?"

"I would if I could," Moore said. "I did, in fact, say something to Mr. Hoyt, but he seemed to have no desire to follow my suggestion."

"Oh, well—*dum spiro, spero*. Good day, gentlemen." He walked out, headed toward the front door.

"Now, what do you suppose he said?" Moore said, staring after the departing professor.

"It was Latin," I said. " 'While I breathe, I hope.' "

Moore turned and stared at me. "Now I've heard everything," he said. "A private eye who knows Latin."

"In the first place," I said flatly, "I'm an insurance detective and not a private eye. And I'm getting tired of everybody assuming that you have to be an idiot just because you're in a line like this. How about trotting out your goodies? I want to get this clambake over and get back to my interrupted honeymoon."

"What about Miss Holden?" he asked.

"Let her go find her own honeymoon," I said. "Come on. Let's get this show on the road."

"All right," he said. "You want to see all this stuff?"

"Not necessarily, but I suppose I'd better look at enough to see what's involved."

"I'm told," Moore said, "that each of these cases also has an alarm connected to it as well as being locked. You might check with Swanson. Here's the diary, if you're interested."

I looked down through the glass at the small book resting in the center of the case. A white card identified it as "The diary of Mary Kennerley Hanna, 1780–1830." That was all. The book was closed. It seemed to have a leather cover, but this was so faded and cracked that it was difficult to be sure.

"What's it worth?" I asked curiously.

"Probably nothing," he said. "Depending on what's in it, it might be valuable, but the mere age doesn't make it worth anything. Since I haven't seen the contents, I appraised it at one dollar."

"Guess nobody will steal it, then," I said, "unless the professor gets tired of waiting."

"These volumes," Moore said, moving to the bookcases, "are a little more valuable. Are you interested in books?"

"I don't mind curling up with a good book if there's nothing better," I said.

"In some cases there are people who might think there is nothing better," he said. "For example, here"—he tapped on the glass to indicate a faded book—"is a copy of *Lyrical Ballads* by William Wordsworth and Samuel T. Coleridge. It was published by Biggs and Cottle in London in 1798. This copy contains the canceled leaves bearing the poem 'Lewti; or The Circassian Love Chant' as well as the leaves with 'The Nightingale,' which replaced it in later editions. It's worth about seven thousand dollars."*

"That's a lot of money to curl up with," I admitted.

"And here's a copy of *Poems: Written by Wil. Shakespeare, Gent.* It contains a portrait of Shakespeare by William Marshall. It was printed in London in 1640 by Thomas Cotes, although the binding was added sometime in the eighteenth century. Worth something over five thousand dollars."

I laughed. "That proves Shakespeare was wrong when he said, 'Words pay no debts.' "

Moore looked at me. "Latin and Shakespeare quotations," he said.

"I also have all the vices," I said. "Stop gushing over me as if I had two heads. Any more big-money books?"

"A few," he said. "Here's a first edition of *Gulliver's Travels* by Jonathan Swift, published in London in 1726. *The Countess of Pembroke's Arcadia,* by Sir Philip Sidney, printed in London in 1590. A multivolume translation of Homer, by George Chapman, printed in 1610. Poems by Robert Burns, published in 1786. Benjamin Franklin's *M.T. Cicero's Cato Major, or His Discourse of Old Age,* published by Franklin in

---

* About $65,000 in today's money.

1774. Those are the biggest items, but there are many, many books here—like *An Inquiry into the Nature and Causes of the Wealth of Nations* by Adam Smith, published in London in 1776—which are worth from fifty to two hundred dollars each."

"No pornography?" I asked in mock disappointment.

His mouth tightened automatically, but he finally managed a grin. "None in the Coonskin Library," he said. "They lived pretty lustily in those days, so I don't think they needed it. I'll just show you a couple more things."

"Good," I said.

"Most of these cases," he said, waving around the room, "are filled with glassware. Some of it was made by Caspar Wistar in New Jersey, sometime before the Revolution. The rest was made by John Frederick Amelung of New Bremen, Maryland, between 1787 and 1795. Now, here's a rare silver pine-tree shilling made in 1652 by John Hull of Massachusetts."

I looked through the glass at the tarnished silver coin. It didn't look like much. "I don't keep up with the rate of exchange," I said, "but I'd offer twenty cents for it." He laughed without humor. "Here," he said, tapping on another case, "is probably the prize discovery among all these things."

I glanced through the glass and saw a silver bowl. There seemed to be considerable etching around it. A white card identified it as being loaned by Miss Malvyna Hanna.

"Until this was discovered," Moore said, "only one of these bowls was known to be in existence—in the possession of the Museum of Fine Arts in Boston. Now we know that a pair was made. This is known as the Sons of Liberty Bowl and has been called the most historic piece of American silver. It was made by Paul Revere in 1768 to commemorate defiance of royal authority by members of the Massachusetts House of Representatives. The etching around the bowl states that it is to the memory of the glorious ninety-two who voted not to rescind a protest to King George III against measures restricting trade."

For the first time I was impressed. It was a beautiful piece of work. Some of this must have shown in my face, for Moore chuckled.

"I'm glad to see that you are not indifferent to all of what Mr. Kryle calls junk," he said. "Now I suppose you'd like to see the special policeman?"

I nodded.

"If I can judge by my visit yesterday," he said, "we'll find him in the kitchen, drinking beer." He led the way through a door into a large kitchen.

There was a table and several chairs against one wall. A man was sitting at one end, a glass of beer in front of him. He was slumped down in his chair, but as I got a good look at him, I saw that he was a big man. He wore a blue uniform, a little like a cop's, with a special badge. A holster with gun was buckled to his hip. He looked between thirty-five and forty. His face was heavy, without much expression.

His glance raked over me and finally settled on my companion. "The insurance man," he said. His voice was a rumbling monotone with no more expression than his face.

"That's right," Moore said. "This is Milo March, also of the insurance company. Milo, this is Fred Swanson, the special policeman hired by Crescent."

"Howdy," Fred Swanson said. He offered me a beefy hand.

"Mr. March is here to look at the security measures."

The policeman nodded. "Beer?" he asked.

"No, thanks," I said. "I'm strictly a whiskey man myself. You on duty, Swanson?"

"Nope," he said. He pulled a heavy watch from his pocket and looked at it. "Don't go on duty until five o'clock. From five at night until five in the morning." His eyes raked me over again. "You an insurance dick?"

"You might call me that. How come you're here if you're not on duty?"

"I live here with Enoch. I always get into the uniform in the middle of the afternoon and take it easy till five."

"Then you're on guard here from five at night until five in the morning?"

"Yeah."

"And sometimes you're around during the day?"

"Yeah. I usually sleep till twelve or one. Then if I ain't got anything else to do, I'm here the rest of the time."

"And if you're not? What's the guard arrangement then, during the day?"

"Well, Enoch is always here. He ain't a special cop, but he's got a gun, and I guess he can shoot just as straight as if he was."

"That's all?"

He took a drink of beer and wiped the back of his hand across his mouth. "The city cops make a point of coming by every couple of hours and they're by every hour at night. Chief McArdle gave orders for that as soon as this place was opened."

"What about alarms?" I asked.

"There are alarms on all the doors and windows, and there are other alarms on all the glass cases."

"Alarms connected directly to the police department?"

"No. Regular burglar alarms. But they can be heard for several blocks, and somebody would call the cops if they didn't hear it themselves."

"They're turned off part of the time?" I asked.

"The ones on the doors and windows are turned off during the day. The ones on the cases are never turned off."

"Who turns them off and on?"

"Enoch turns them off in the morning around nine o'clock when he opens up. I turn them on at night when I go on duty."

"Okay," I said. "You had any experience as a guard?"

"Some."

"Know how to use that gun you're carrying?"

His eyes locked with mine. "I know how to use it," he said flatly.

"I'm sure you do," I said. My private thought was that he'd probably enjoy an opportunity. "Well, I'll see you around, Fred."

"Yeah," he said, and went back to his beer.

Lionel Moore and I went out of the house. We didn't see anything of Enoch Drake.

"Now we have a choice," Moore said. "We can telephone for a cab or we can walk back to the hotel."

"How far?" I asked.

"About eight blocks."

"You know where the police station is?"

"Not exactly, but I think it's only a block or so away from the hotel."

"We might as well walk, then," I said. "We can probably make it while we're waiting for the taxi. Besides, the driver will want to start a long conversation with us. Let's go."

His estimate was close. It was nine blocks, and it didn't take us long to make it.

"Anything more you want from me?" he asked.

"I don't think so," I said. "It'll be up to the office to put our two reports together and make up their minds. You've already made your report?"

"Wrote it out last night and mailed it. You're going to talk to the local police?"

"Yeah."

"Well, good luck," he said. "I'll probably be checked out by the time you get back. I'm off for home."

"Where's that?"

"They sent me down from Cleveland."

"How are you traveling?"

"My own car."

"Lucky guy," I said. "Well, I won't be long after you. I'm going to check with the police, come back, and write up my report. Then I'll either catch that six-fifty train tonight to Cincinnati and take a plane from there, or take a cab to Columbus and get a plane."

"Well, good luck," he said. He held out his hand.

"You, too," I said. I grinned at him. "Better stay away from the high priestess if you want to get back."

He laughed nervously. "Don't worry, I will. I might give you the same advice."

"I like what's waiting for me better," I said. "Wild horses couldn't keep me in this town later than this afternoon."

I waved to him and went on up the street. I stopped someone on the corner and asked about the police station. "Around the corner on Washington Street," I was told. I turned left and walked down the street. I almost passed it before I realized I'd arrived. I went in and soon got directed to the office of the Chief of Police.

Chief John McArdle was a middle-aged, heavyset man who looked a lot like a politician except that his eyes looked more intelligent. I introduced myself and showed him my identification.

"Glad to know you, March," he said. He sounded as if he might mean it. I was surprised. Cops usually bristle at the mention of "insurance investigator." Maybe they were outside his experience and that's why he was friendly. "What can I do for you?"

"Just answer a few questions," I said. "I have to make a report to the insurance company on the security arrangements for that Crescent Museum."

"You can tell them," he said dryly, "that I'm not very happy about it. We don't have much that you could call crime in Athens, but I don't like the idea of something that valuable lying around."

"I can understand that," I said.

He shifted around in his chair and lit a cigar. "I don't know much about big-city crime, but I got an idea if anybody come around to collect that stuff, they just might get away with it. I'd like to put a closer watch on it, but I just ain't got the force. I have a night man out in a car, and I've told him to go by every hour, but I can't do more than that. He's got to cover the rest of the town or there'd be hell to pay."

"Let's take it for granted," I said, "that you owe more to the citizens of the town than you do to either Crescent Pictures or my insurance company."

He looked surprised. "I kind of figured you'd feel different," he said. "Figured the insurance company would start screaming because I didn't put twenty or thirty men on it. Them picture people did."

"It's a little unguarded," I said, thinking this was one of the understatements of the year. "But the picture company can afford to hire more than one guard. I will recommend that they'd better if they want to keep the policy. Anyway, Chief, they probably have a bigger budget than your town has. What do you know about this guy they have hired?"

"Fred Swanson? Fred's all right. A little on the lazy side, but that's all. Ain't done much since he came back from the war, but I've used him three, four times when I've had to swear in extra men. The county sheriff's used him as a special deputy a few times, and that's about all he's done. Fred'll never set the world on fire, but I'd say he's honest enough."

I nodded. "Know anything about the burglar alarms they're using?"

"Good ones. They'll make enough racket they could probably be heard here."

"One more question, Chief, and I'll leave you. What about Enoch Drake?"

He scratched his head. "Enoch's another one a little like Fred. He's never had any more to do with work than he had to. Some of them things belong to him, and as for the rest, he's lived around furniture like that most of his life, so I expect it's a little hard for Enoch to really believe all that stuff is as valuable as it is. In that respect I guess Enoch might be a little careless, but I'd say he's honest. Never heard anything against him."

"Thanks," I said, standing up. I grinned at him. "I don't suppose you have much of a crime wave around here?"

"Not much," he admitted, "but it's as much as we want. But from now on, I'm going to keep an eye out for strangers."

"It's a good idea," I said. "Thanks again."

"Glad to help," he said. "You expect to be around long?"

"Not me," I said. "I'm going to be out of here within a few hours." I turned and left.

It was after four when I finally got back to the hotel. I realized I hadn't had anything to eat since about eleven, so I went into the coffee shop and had some lunch.

On the way back I stopped at the desk. I asked about Ernesto. There was a message for me from Curtis Hoyt, the Hollywood writer. It said that he'd taken Ernesto out and they'd be back about five. I asked the clerk to tell them I'd be in my room. Then I arranged with the clerk to have a public stenographer sent up to my room. At first he looked a little dubious, so I told him I'd be willing to leave my door open. Then he got indignant at my thinking that he would think what he was thinking. But he promised to do it.

It was five by the time I got to my room. I could see I wasn't going to catch the train, so I'd have to go by taxi to Columbus.

Before the stenographer arrived, the phone rang and it was Hoyt. He and Ernesto were down in the lobby. He said that Ernesto was hungry and wanted to know if there was time to get him something.

"Ernesto is always hungry," I told him. "But there's time. I'll be busy on my report for about two hours."

"That'll be good timing," Hoyt said. "I usually go over to the museum to work on the script about eight. I'll keep Ernesto busy until you're through."

"Good," I said. "How's he doing?"

"You should know," he said. "Kids like Ernesto do all right wherever they go. I've been showing him the town. I had a little trouble keeping him from starting a crap game on the floor of the post office, but otherwise everything's been fine. See you later."

He hung up, and a moment later the public stenographer arrived. The clerk needn't have worried about sending her to my room. She was at least forty and looked every minute of it.

I started dictating my report, giving all the details on everything. A lot of this was not so much facts as a personal evaluation. It seemed to me that, on the face of it, the stuff would normally be pretty safe in Athens even though there weren't enough guards for a million-dollar policy. On the other hand, I knew that the picture company would wring every drop of publicity they could out of the matter. There wasn't much danger of anybody coming down and walking out with the furniture under his coat. But other things, like some of the books, the Paul Revere bowl, and maybe even the glassware, might attract some crooks from anywhere in the country. It was stuff like that the insurance company wanted. So I gave it to them.

When I finally finished, the stenographer went off to type it up. She promised to rush. I went into the bathroom and showered and shaved. Then I put on some clean clothes and sat down to wait.

Ernesto showed up at a little after seven. He had obviously had a good time. He'd also learned some new English, which he insisted on displaying. In addition to "okay," he now knew "damn," "hot dog," "crumb bum," and a couple of short words which had been popular, but clandestine, since the days of the Angles and the Saxons. I carefully explained to him that he wasn't to make public use of the latter. There was no point in being angry at the writer; Ernesto had probably only tried to learn the English equivalents of some of his favorite words in Spanish, and Hoyt had obligingly provided them.

At eight o'clock the stenographer returned with the typed report. I checked it and paid her. I put it in an envelope and addressed it to John Franklin in New York, via air mail and special delivery. Then I put in a call to the airport at Columbus. I could get a plane to Denver at eleven o'clock. I called the taxi company and they said they could get me there in time to get on the plane. The driver would pick me up at eight-thirty.

It was twenty-five after eight by the time Ernesto and I were ready to go downstairs. I took a last look around the room to be sure we weren't leaving anything.

"The woman will meet us?" Ernesto asked.

"Not 'the woman,' " I said. "She's going to be your mother, but I think it will be all right if you call her Greta if it's going to make you feel unmanly to call her Mother."

He made a face which indicated his opinion of the entire female sex. "We will live in a palace, Don Milo?"

"Hardly a palace," I said. "It's a five-room apartment. But it's large enough so you'll have your own room."

"A room to myself?" he exclaimed. "Then it is truly a palace. It is as I have said: you are a rich man, Don Milo."

"Don't tell my creditors," I said. "Come on, Ernesto. We don't want to miss the plane." I started for the door.

The telephone rang.

I thought it was the clerk calling to tell me the taxi was waiting. I picked up the receiver and said hello.

"Milo?" an excited voice asked. I didn't recognize it.

"Yeah," I said.

"This is Curtis Hoyt," he said. "Boy, am I glad I caught you. There's hell to pay."

"If you have anything to say, say it fast," I told him. "I'm on my way to catch a plane."

"Not now," he said. "Enoch Drake has been murdered, and a lot of stuff is missing from the museum."

For a moment I didn't get it. I'd been considering this a routine investigation, and with it over, my thoughts were entirely on getting back to Denver and Greta. The idea that anything could actually happen was so far from my mind that the words of Curtis Hoyt simply didn't penetrate at once. When they did, I wished they hadn't.

"Oh, no," I said.

"Yes," he said. "I got down here at a quarter to eight and found the front door wide open. When I got inside, I found the old man dead and a lot of cases smashed open."

I looked at my watch. It was eight-thirty.

"At a quarter to eight?" I said. "What the hell have you been doing for the last forty-five minutes?"

"Making phone calls," he said. "I called Crescent in Hollywood the first thing, then I phoned the police. Then I thought I'd better call you, too."

I had a sinking feeling.

"Look, Hoyt," I said hurriedly, "do me a favor, will you? Pretend that you didn't make this call. I'm going—"

There was a click as the operator cut in on us. "I'm sorry, Mr. March," she said. "There's a long-distance call for you from New York. He says that it's urgent."

"I'll see you later, Milo," Hoyt said. I heard him hang up.

"Just a minute, operator," I said desperately. "About that call from New York. Tell them you can't locate me and—"

"Don't waste your time, Milo," a new voice cut in. "I'm already on the line and I can hear you." I recognized this voice all right. It was John Franklin in New York.

I groaned to myself. I knew what was happening, but I didn't understand how or why. But I still tried.

"Look, John," I said hurriedly, "I've just mailed the report to you and I'm on my way to catch a plane. I don't have time to talk to you now. I'll—"

"Don't hang up," he said sharply. "If you do, you'll be through in the insurance business for the rest of your life."

"You're a son-of-a-bitch," I said bitterly.

"I'm sorry, Milo," he said in a softer tone. "I know how you feel, but you know damn well you can't run out on a case when it's happened right under your nose. I wasn't threatening you; I was just stating a fact. You know how your agency and my Board of Directors would act—would have to act—if you ran out on this."

"You know what's happened?" I asked.

"Yes."

"How the hell did you find out? It's only been forty-five minutes since it was discovered."

"Somebody reported it to Crescent Pictures in Hollywood. Apparently they were also told that you were on the spot and about to leave, because they burned up the wires locating me. I just finished talking to them and put in the call to you. All I know is that the guard or somebody has been killed and a number of the insured items stolen. Is there any more to it?"

That Hollywood writer, I thought. Why couldn't he stick to writing? If he hadn't been in such a hurry to call his studio, or if he'd called me first, I would have been out of town.

"That's all I know," I said shortly, "except that Alexander Graham Bell should have minded his own business."

He laughed. "That sounds more like you, Milo," he said. "Like I said before, I'm sorry as hell this has happened, but it has and there's nothing else we can do about it. That's a small town, so you ought to be able to clean it up fast and get back to your bride."

"Oh, sure."

"It shouldn't be hard for you," he said. "You can leave the murder to the local cops, but find the stolen stuff. If you get it all back, you can go home."

"Thanks for nothing," I said.

"I'll call Inter-World," he said. "Need any money?"

"Yeah. Wire me a thousand dollars."

"A thousand dollars? In that little town? What do you need that much for?"

"I'm going to bribe someone to confess," I snapped. "Just send me the money."

"All right," he said. "Good luck. Clean it up fast and give my love to your bride when you see her."

"When I see her," I said bitterly. "I'll be lucky if she doesn't sue me for divorce." I slammed the receiver down.

"*Qué hay?*" Ernesto asked.

"What's up?" I repeated. "I am. Up the creek without a paddle. We're stuck here."

"*Qué pasa?*"

"A man has been murdered and a number of things stolen."

His face lit up. "Then we go to work, is it not so?"

"No, it is not so," I said. *"We* do not go to work. *I* go to work. You are going to stay here and go to bed within the next hour."

His face fell. "To bed? Why? I am not sick, Don Milo."

"You're going to get some new habits in America, Ernesto. I know that in Madrid you stayed up half the night. Here boys of your age go to bed by nine o'clock so they can get enough sleep."

"It is not manly," he protested.

"Nevertheless that's the way it is," I said firmly. I was aware that I was directing some of my anger toward Ernesto, but I also knew that I had to start changing his habits. "Maybe you can stick around tomorrow, but not tonight."

He went over and threw himself on the bed. *"Es el colmo,"* he muttered, which might be roughly translated as saying "That's the last straw."

I grinned at him. "Relax, Ernesto," I said. *"Todo saldrá en la colada."*

"Déjame en paz," he said sullenly.

He was acting like any other boy who had to go to bed when he didn't want to, but I knew that he'd get over it. I started to reach for the phone, but it beat me to it by ringing. I picked it up and said hello. It was the operator. She said that Chief of Police McArdle was in the lobby wanting to see me.

"Tell him I'll be right down," I said. "In the meantime, I want to put in a call to Denver." I gave her the number at my apartment.

In a few minutes I had Greta on the phone. I told her what

had happened. She was disappointed, but I must admit that she took it better than I did.

"I'm sorry, darling," she said, "but if that's the way it is, there isn't much we can do about it. How long do you think it will take you?"

"I don't know," I said. "This town is small enough so that we ought to be able to search the whole place in a few hours. But who knows."

"I'll be waiting for you," she said. "How's Ernesto?"

"He's sulking now because I won't let him go with me tonight. The Chief of Police is waiting for me down in the lobby."

"Better not keep him waiting, then," she said. "I miss you, darling."

"No more than I miss you. And I'm going to turn this town upside down. Maybe it won't be more than a day or two."

It took us a few more dozen words to say good-bye, but we finally made it. I put the receiver down and headed for the door.

"*Hasta luego,*" I called over my shoulder to Ernesto. "Don't forget—to bed and to sleep."

"*Váyase a paseo,*" he snapped.

Downstairs the Chief was pacing back and forth in the lobby.

"Figured I'd stop by for you," he said as I came up. "Thought you might like getting a ride over to the place."

"I don't like going," I said, "but thanks."

"It's your job to work on it, isn't it?" he asked as we walked out to his car.

"I'm stuck with it, if that's what you mean," I said. "I was just on the point of leaving when they got me on the phone. Another two minutes and I would have been gone. That shows you what kind of luck I have."

He glanced at me as he started the motor. "Don't want to work on it?"

"Not now," I said. I unbent enough to explain it. "I was just married yesterday morning and was about to start my honeymoon when I was dragged off to New York. Before I could get out of there, I was shipped out here. Now I'm stuck for who knows how long."

He chuckled. "Sorry, son," he said. "I know it ain't funny for you, but you got to admit it's a little humorous to outsiders."

"I suppose so," I admitted.

"Why not bring her out here? It's a nice, quiet place, and you could have a little honeymoon while not working."

"Not my idea of a honeymoon. Besides, I'm hoping that it won't take that long to turn the stuff up. We ought to dig it up pretty quick, don't you think?"

"Maybe," he said, but he didn't seem to be going overboard for it. "Maybe not. Don't know what we'll find. I reckon I'm sorry you're getting your private life all messed up this way, but I'll admit I'm kind of glad you're here."

I looked at him in surprise. It was the first time I could ever remember a police official welcoming the presence of an insurance investigator.

"That's a switch," I said. "Cops usually don't like to have anybody peering over their shoulders."

"You just been dealing with the wrong cops, son," he said, chuckling again. "I figure I do a pretty good job policing this town, and I don't know as I'd want you to tell me how to run my force. But this thing tonight looks like it come out of an insurance deal. That's something you've had more experience with, so I figure you can make it easier for me."

"I hope you're right," I said. I lit a cigarette and puffed on it nervously. I'd simmered down enough to think about working, but I was still angry about the whole situation. "You got any ideas yet, Chief?"

"Don't know any more'n you do, I expect," he said. "One of my men is over there, and I guess the Coroner will be there by the time we arrive. I was out with my wife and they had to track me down. All I know is that somebody bashed Enoch Drake in the head and walked off with some of the stuff. Heard you'd been notified, too."

"Notified, hell," I said. "That Hollywood writer discovered the murder. The first thing he did was call his studio in Hollywood. He told them I was here and about ready to leave town. They called New York and screamed at the insurance company. They called Athens and caught me just as I was ready to walk out of the room."

The Chief chuckled. "Smart boy," he said.

"Too damn smart," I grunted.

We did no more talking until we reached the house. There were a number of people crowded around the sidewalk in front of the house. The Chief parked the car and we pushed through the crowd. Several people spoke to the Chief, but he merely grunted back at them. We opened the front door of the house and walked in.

There was no one in the first room, but we could hear voices in the room beyond it and we went on back. We stepped into the room where I had seen the books and the glass-covered cases. There were four men there—that is, four who were alive.

One of the cases had crashed over on the floor and there was broken glass all around it. Near it the body of Enoch Drake was sprawled. He was face down and I could see the crushed, bloody spot on the back of his head.

A thin, elderly man was down on one knee near the body, staring at the wound. He looked as if he didn't enjoy the job.

Fred Swanson, the special policeman, and Curtis Hoyt were standing watching him. The policeman was shifting around and looking uncomfortable. Hoyt seemed to be enjoying himself—maybe because he was in the middle of something instead of merely writing about it.

The fourth man was a young policeman who came forward as we entered the room. I got the impression that he was glad to see his chief.

"Hello, Walt," the Chief said. "Everything all right?"

"Yes, sir," the young policeman said uncertainly. He glanced at me questioningly.

"This is Milo March from the insurance company," the Chief said. "Milo, shake hands with Walt Sawyer." The young cop and I shook hands.

"Hello, Ben," the Chief said. The man kneeling on the floor looked up. "Ben, this is Milo March from the insurance company. This is Ben Chapman, our coroner." The Coroner nodded at me, his gaze jumping back to the Chief. "I'm glad you're here, John. This is a nasty business."

"Looks like it," Chief McArdle said. He looked around the room and his gaze finally came to rest on the special policeman. Swanson seemed to shrink under the gaze. "You on duty tonight, Fred?"

"Yeah," the big man mumbled.

"Thought you was. Maybe you were in the can when this happened?" His voice was so gentle that it took me a couple of seconds to realize that he was being ironical.

The big man squirmed. "Nope. I wasn't in the house."

"On duty somewhere else?"

"No. I went down the street to get a cup of coffee. I did that lots of times when Enoch and I didn't feel like making coffee. Enoch said it was all right."

"Nice of him," the Chief said, looking down at the body. "What time did you go out for this coffee?"

"Seven-thirty."

"When did you get back?"

"A quarter past eight."

"After the murder and after it had been discovered?"

"Yeah."

"A big cup of coffee," Chief McArdle said.

The big man squirmed some more. "I guess maybe I had some pie, and I was talking some to Millie, the waitress. I didn't know there was any reason to hurry back."

"I've heard," the Chief said softly, "that murderers don't often announce their plans in advance. The point is, Fred, you was supposed to be on duty here. Not in a coffee shop."

"It was Enoch who told me to go," Fred Swanson said defensively. "When he didn't feel like making coffee, he'd want me to go. I'd always bring him back some coffee—and some for Mr. Hoyt here, since he's been coming over every night."

"Bring them some tonight?"

"Yeah. In the kitchen. I guess it's cold now."

"So's Enoch," the Chief said. He looked at the writer. "You're Hoyt, the fellow that called me?"

"Yes," Hoyt said. He took off his glasses and began polishing them with his handkerchief. His eyes were shining with excitement. "I don't think we've met, but I've seen you around town since we've been here. I'm Curtis Hoyt. I'm writing the script on the picture we're going to do here."

The Chief nodded. "You got here at what time?"

"About a quarter to eight, maybe ten minutes to. The door was standing open "

"We'll get your full story in a minute," the Chief interrupted. "If Fred left at seven-thirty and you got here fifteen or twenty minutes later, that kind of pins it down. How long you figure he's been dead, Ben?"

The Coroner looked up, pursing his lips. "Sounds about right," he said. He didn't sound as if he knew what he was talking about.

"What do you think, Walt?" the Chief asked, turning to the young cop. Something in his voice gave me the idea that it was Walt's answer he was interested in rather than the Coroner's.

"It can't be really pinned down that close," the young cop

said. "I'd say he'd been dead between one and two hours, and that time would fit in. It's now a quarter past nine."

The Chief nodded and looked at me. "Walt is our prize cop," he said. "He studied up in Columbus. But most of the time we got no call for his special talents." He turned back to the Coroner. "What do you think, Ben?"

"It was murder, all right," the Coroner said pompously. He stood up and I saw he was tall. Tall and skinny. "He was hit in the back of the head. With that." He pointed to the floor and I saw a heavy poker. The end of it was black with blood. It was bent a little. "Hit him so hard looks like it crushed his head. Bent the poker, too. I'd say Enoch never knew what hit him."

The Chief glanced at the young cop and he nodded his head. "Must have hit him pretty hard to bend that poker. Where'd it come from?"

It was Fred Swanson who answered. "From one of the other rooms. There's some old andirons and stuff in there that belongs to Mrs. Singer. That was with them."

"Anybody touch anything?" the Chief asked. He was looking at Hoyt and Fred Swanson.

"No," they both said again.

"I guess maybe we can move into the kitchen in a minute, Walt, and let you get to work. You got everything?" The young cop nodded, and I noticed a leather bag sitting on the floor. Next to it there was a camera.

The Chief saw me looking. "All modern equipment," he said with pride. "Any way we tell right off what's been taken?"

"I can give you a rough idea," Curtis Hoyt said. "At least from this room, but I imagine that's all. They wouldn't have had time to carry out much furniture. The diary is gone, for one thing."

"Who'd want somebody's old diary?" the Chief asked in surprise.

"I think it might be pretty valuable," Hoyt said. "Then the silver pine shilling is gone and so is the silver bowl that was made by Paul Revere. The glass on all three cases was broken. I don't think any of the glassware's been taken. But the glass on the bookcases has been kicked in, and I think some of the books are gone."

I walked over and looked at the bookcases. Two panels of glass were broken. I leaned down and looked at the shelf where Moore had earlier pointed out some of the books. It was obvious that some volumes were missing.

"I can't be sure about the others," I said, "but I can tell now that at least two books aren't here that I saw this afternoon. One was a book of poems by Shakespeare and the other poems by Wordsworth and Coleridge."

"Poetry thieves," the Coroner snorted.

"I think Moore said that those two volumes alone were worth about twelve thousand dollars," I said. "And that's the kind of stuff you can easily get rid of. A lot of collectors are glad to buy without asking any questions."

"How about the coin and the bowl?" the Chief asked. "Moore didn't say what they were worth, but I'm sure it's plenty. He did say that the bowl was the most valuable thing here."

"What about other things?" the Chief asked. "Ain't you got a list of everything here?"

"Not me," I said. "There'd be no point to my having a list. Moore probably sent a list to the New York office. Then there'd be one with the policy, and I suppose the studio has one in Hollywood. We can send to New York for one, but why can't the owners check over their stuff and see what's missing?"

"The women can, but Enoch was one of the owners. I don't reckon he ever kept a list of anything."

"I just thought of something," Hoyt said. "Lili Robben has a list of everything here."

"Who's she?"

"The research girl who's with us. She's had a list of everything so we can check it when we want to—for the script or for the prop department. She's at the hotel. Want me to call her?"

"I guess not," the Chief said. "Don't reckon we can do much with it before morning. Let's move into the kitchen so Walt can get to work, and then Ben can get Enoch out of here."

The four of us—the Chief, Fred Swanson, Curtis Hoyt, and I—went into the kitchen. The Chief pulled out a chair and sat down at the table. Hoyt and I joined him. There was a paper bag on the table, probably with the coffee in it.

Fred Swanson stood uncertainly in the middle of the kitchen. "Like to have a beer, Chief?" he asked.

"No. Get one for yourself, Fred, and sit down."

The special cop opened the refrigerator and got a can of beer. He punched two holes in the top and came over to the table.

"Fred," the Chief said, "what happened with the burglar alarms tonight?"

"I don't know," he muttered. "While we was waiting for you to come, I looked around and I saw that the alarms for the cases had been turned off, but the others hadn't been."

"How could you get in without knocking them off?"

"Enoch could let anybody in without them going off. That is, if he opened the door from the inside."

"That's right," Hoyt said. "Every night when I'd arrive, I'd knock on the door and he'd come and peer through the window. As soon as he'd recognize me, he'd open the door."

"Enoch must've let the murderer in," Fred Swanson said. He sounded relieved, as though that took some of the responsibility from his shoulders.

"That's it," Curtis Hoyt said. He sounded excited. "It must have been someone he knew. That ought to narrow it down."

"Maybe," the Chief said. "Maybe it was somebody Enoch knew—but that'd still leave quite a few people. And maybe it was somebody that convinced Enoch they had a good reason to be let inside."

"The first sounds better to me," Hoyt said firmly. I glanced at the Chief and he grinned. It was obvious that the Hollywood writer didn't have a very good opinion of small-town cops—or maybe of any cops.

"Going to solve this yourself?" I asked him.

"I might," he said. "I don't think it should be too difficult."

"In that case," I said, "why the hell did you make such a point of getting me stopped from leaving town?"

He laughed. "I've been writing about private eyes for years," he said, "and I thought it might be nice to see one in action. I want to see if a real one is as smart as the ones in my scripts." Clearly, he didn't think they were.

"I don't much care who solves it as long as it gets done," the Chief said mildly. "Now, Mr. Hoyt, maybe you could tell us about your arrival."

"Sure," Hoyt said. "As I said, I got here about a quarter to eight, maybe ten to, and found the front door open. That was pretty unusual, but at the time I didn't think too much about it. I thought it was just carelessness. I knew that Drake never took any of this stuff very seriously. Even when it came to these old books he owned. I don't think he ever really believed they were worth a lot of money. He always acted as if he'd pulled a fast one on the studio and that sooner or later we'd wake up to the fact that we'd been throwing our money away."

The Chief nodded. "Enoch was like that," he said. "He never figured anything was worth much unless it was in hard cash. He got them books from his father, who was always poorer'n a church mouse, so I guess his idea was if the books was worth anything, the old man would've cashed in on them. Go ahead."

"I found the door open, so I walked in. Everything looked all right, although I didn't see anyone around. I thought maybe Fred had already gotten the coffee and they were in the kitchen. I came back here. I still didn't think anything was wrong. My first idea was that maybe Fred was out for coffee and Enoch was upstairs taking a nap, but I stuck my head in through the door there and then I saw him. I guess maybe I took a quick look around—without touching anything. Then I went to the telephone."

"In the parlor?"

"In that front room, yes."

"Didn't call the police first, did you?" Chief McArdle asked.

"No. As a matter of fact, that wasn't deliberate. It was just that I automatically thought of the studio first. I knew that Milo here was about to leave town and I knew that the studio wouldn't like it if he wasn't on the spot when some of their stuff was missing. Crescent Pictures likes to have action when their money is involved."

"Figured small-town cops wouldn't know how to handle a big-time murder like this, didn't you?" the Chief asked mildly.

Having it pinned down like that didn't bother Hoyt at all. "As a matter of fact," he said calmly, "I did. After all, you don't get a chance for much experience along this line. Anyway, I called Ed Harrow in Hollywood. He's the producer on *West to the Hocking,* and the rental on all this stuff and the cost of the insurance is part of his budget. I told him what had happened and suggested that he ought to move fast so the insurance company could catch Milo before he got out of town."

"You're a gentleman and a scholar and a son-of-a-bitch," I said.

He grinned at me. "Then I called you, Chief—or rather I called the station. Fred came back about that time and I told him what had happened. Then I phoned Milo and told him. After that, Fred and I sat and waited until your cop and the coroner arrived. That's all."

"It's enough," the Chief said heavily. He sounded plaintive as he went on. "I ain't got anything against strangers, but this is one time I wish you people had stayed in Hollywood. These antiques have been around Athens for a hundred and fifty years without anybody being killed over them; you come along and say they're worth a million dollars and right away we got trouble."

"Maybe this is only the first time it was discovered that somebody was murdered," Hoyt said. "This ought to do you a lot of good, Chief. Think of the publicity you'll get."

"I don't need it."

"It ought to be easy to clean up," Hoyt went on. "I don't think that this means any out-of-town hoods came in and grabbed the stuff. It had to be somebody local. It seems to me you ought to be able to narrow it down easily."

"How?" the Chief asked bluntly.

"First," Hoyt said, ticking off a finger, "it must have been somebody Enoch Drake knew, since he let the person in. Secondly, from the fact that the person was able to pick out the few things that were the most valuable, it had to be someone who was familiar with what each thing here is worth."

"That narrows it down to about eight thousand people—ten thousand if you consider the whole county," the Chief said. "The *Athens Messenger* did a story on the museum, at the insistence of someone from your picture company, in which they gave the value of the most important items."

"Well, it still should be easy."

"How long you been coming here in the evenings, Mr. Hoyt?" the Chief asked.

"A week or so."

"Always get here about the same time?"

"Yes. I usually arrive between seven forty-five and eight. Why?"

"Just like to have everything neat-like," the Chief said. He turned to look at the big man sitting at the end of the table. "Fred, looks like you made a little mistake."

"It wasn't my fault," Fred Swanson said defensively. "Enoch told me to go get coffee. He always did. He'd say it was about time for this writing fellow to show up and I'd better go get coffee for all of us."

"Wasn't working for Enoch," the Chief pointed out. "Don't figure the picture company and the insurance company are going to like it." He turned his head to look at me. "That about right?"

"Close to it," I said. "I imagine if the insurance company wanted to be real tough about it, they could claim negligence to cut down on the amount of payment. I don't think, however, they will do that." I lit a cigarette and stared at the big man through the smoke. "But I do think that if we don't find the stuff pretty quick, we may want to ask some more questions about this trip out for coffee. It could mean more than negligence."

Fred Swanson glared at me. "What do you mean by that crack?"

"Just what I said. You could have been after coffee. On the other hand, the coffee could have been an excuse to leave Enoch Drake and the house unguarded while a friend of yours came around. Enoch would have been just as apt to let a friend of yours in as one of his own."

He gripped the edge of the table and half raised up out of his chair. "You got no call to say I had anything to do with it," he said hoarsely. "I got a good mind—"

"In the first place," I said evenly, "you don't have a good mind. You and Enoch were both idiots, only he's a dead one. Now, sit down."

"Smart insurance dick," he said. He was gripping the table so hard the knuckles of his hands were white. "I can take you."

"Maybe," I said. I wanted to reach over and smash him in the face, but I knew this was partly because I was still angry at being stuck there. I'd been wanting to take it out on somebody all along. "You can try anytime you like, Swanson. Only I come expensive to anybody who wants to take me. I don't think you can afford it." I deliberately blew smoke across the table into his face.

He stared at me for a full minute, but he didn't have what it takes. His gaze dropped and he slid back down on his chair, his fingers slowly unclamping from the table.

Curtis Hoyt laughed explosively. "That's what I've been waiting to see," he said. "Some real private-eye stuff. Only you ought to let me give you some new lines. Bogart lines. You'd lay them in the aisles then."

"I'll do my own laying, if you don't mind," I said flatly. He was a little too flip for my taste just then.

"Terrific," he said. He leaned forward, peering at me through his glasses. There was something like malice in his face. "But don't let Niki Holden hear you say that." The Chief cleared his throat to indicate he was taking over.

"Like I said, Fred," he said, "it looks bad for you. About the best you can expect is to lose your job."

"To hell with the job. I didn't do nothing."

"Maybe. You left for coffee about seven-thirty?"

"About that. I didn't mark down the exact time."

"You went to the restaurant down the street—Pierce's—and had coffee and pie?"

"That's right."

"See anybody around when you left the house?"

"Nope. Maybe there was a car or two going by on the street, but that was all."

"I guess you didn't specially look to see if there was anybody hanging around?"

"I didn't make a point of it, but there wasn't anybody."

"Don't you think," the Chief said, "since you was going off when you should've been on duty that you might've looked more carefully?"

"Why?" Swanson asked defensively. "Who the hell would want to steal a lot of old junk?"

"Somebody did," the Chief said gently. "So you had coffee and pie and talked to Millie?"

"I already told you I did."

"While somebody was killing Enoch."

"I didn't have no way of knowing that."

"Didn't say you did," Chief McArdle said. "What did you talk about, you and Millie?"

"Just kidded around."

"And then?"

"Millie made up the containers of coffee for me to bring

back. I paid her and come back here, like always."

"Getting here about a quarter after eight?"

"Yeah."

"Didn't see nobody hanging around when you come back?"

"Nope."

"You go out and get coffee every night this week that Mr. Hoyt's been coming around?"

"Yeah."

"Go about the same time every night?"

"Yeah. Enoch always told me to get it so we'd have it about the time he got here. Maybe sometimes I went a little earlier or later, but not much."

"Enoch sent you?"

"That's what I said."

"Guess Enoch can't tell us no different now."

Fred Swanson glared at the Chief. "You got no right to keep acting as if I done something," he shouted. "You and that smart insurance dick. I'm telling you how it happened."

"Hold your horses," the Chief said. "I was just talking out loud."

"I think Fred is correct," Curtis Hoyt said. "I think it was Enoch who always insisted on getting coffee by the time I got here. I think it was mostly because he wanted it himself, but I was a good excuse for him to send Fred for it."

"Sure," the Chief said. "How come you were over here every night, Mr. Hoyt?"

"I've been working," the writer said. "That old diary Enoch had—the one that's missing—had a lot of good stuff in it which I've been using for a major rewrite of the script. I couldn't come in and examine it during the day when the museum was open. So I've been coming over and making notes from eight to about ten. After that I go back and work on the script until two or three in the morning."

"Uh-huh," the Chief said. He looked at me again. "Anything you want to ask them?"

"You pretty well covered it," I said. "There's just one thing I'd like to know. Were there many people coming in to see the exhibit during the day?"

"Fred?" the Chief prompted.

"I wasn't always here in the day, and when I was, sometimes I was asleep," Fred Swanson said. "All I know is what Enoch said. The first few days there was a lot of people over from the college, but outside of them, there wasn't any more'n one or two people a day. Enoch said it just went to prove that Athens wasn't full of fools."

"Did Enoch show them around or just let them wander around by themselves?"

"He showed them around. He had a regular spiel worked up. He used to sit around at night snickering about it."

"Nothing else I want to ask just now," I told the Chief.

The door swung open and the young cop and the coroner came in.

"Well," the Coroner said, "Walt got through and I had the body taken away. Guess we'll hold the inquest tomorrow, but there ain't any doubt about it he was murdered." The Coroner seemed a little happier now that he wasn't bending over the bloodied corpse.

"I reckon that's all right," the Chief said.

"Figured out anything on it yet?" the Coroner asked.

"Nope."

"I been thinking about it. Want to hear what I think?"

"Sure, Ben," the Chief said. But the way he sounded to me, I thought he didn't care what the Coroner thought but was too polite to say so.

"That young fellow," the Coroner said, nodding in the direction of Hoyt, "was telling me about this professor from the university who's been down here every day wanting to see that old diary. Enoch wouldn't let him see it and the professor was madder'n a wet hen. That diary is one of the things missing."

"Meaning that the professor killed Enoch?"

"Well, I wouldn't want to go so far as to name him, you understand, John. But you know who that professor is?"

"Who is he?"

"Fellow named Rheames. I've heard things about him."

"I expect you have, Ben."

"I don't go for no loose talking," the Coroner said grimly, "but that one's a queer one for fact. Ain't like the other professors. He come down here from Harvard or someplace like that. He's always talking up pretty big against that Senator McCarthy and people like that. It wouldn't surprise me at all if that Rheames was a Communist. Wouldn't surprise some others, either. You ought to keep that in mind, John. Something like this thing tonight just might be done by one of them Communists."

"I see what you mean," the Chief said. "You know me, Ben. I don't want Communists running around here any more'n

I do murderers. Now, if you'd like to swear out a complaint against this professor, I'll be glad to run him in."

"No, no," the Coroner said hurriedly. "I wasn't charging him with anything, you understand. Man may be perfectly all right for all I know. I was just telling you what I've heard—figured it might be of some help. Well, I guess I'd better run along."

"See you tomorrow, Ben," the Chief said. He waited until the Coroner had scuttled down the hallway, then glanced at the young cop. They grinned at each other. "How'd you make out, Walt?"

"Okay, I guess," the young cop said. "I took pictures of every angle of the corpse and of the room. Went over everything for prints too. Got a lot of them, but I don't think it'll do us much good."

"Why?"

"Well, take that poker, for example. Lots of prints on it, but they were mostly smeared as though the last person to handle it had been wearing gloves. So I expect there won't be any prints of the murderer—at least, not any that were left tonight."

"You want to take all of our prints?" Curtis Hoyt asked.

"Tomorrow'll be soon enough," the Chief said. He heaved himself up out of the chair. "I'll send a couple of men over to spend the night here. Can't tell, the murderer might decide to come back and take a crack at Fred." Fred Swanson glared at the hint that he needed protection, but he didn't say anything. "Walt, you stay on until they get here."

"Okay, Chief."

"I guess that's all for tonight. You coming along with me, Milo?"

"Yes," I said.

"Guess I might as well be going back to the hotel, too," Curtis Hoyt said pointedly.

He was wasting his time. "We'll get in touch with you there when we want you," the Chief said. He turned and walked out. I followed him.

He chuckled when we were getting in the car. "Expect I hurt that young fellow's feelings," he said, "but it doesn't pay to get too friendly with anybody when a case is just starting."

"The only reason he wanted to come along," I said, "was so that he could tell us how dumb we are."

"Did seem kind of sure of himself," the Chief said. "You know, son, I like the way you work."

"I didn't do any work yet," I said. "You covered the ground so well there tonight, there wasn't anything for me to do." If we weren't careful, the Chief and I were going to start sounding like a mutual admiration society.

"I meant with Fred," he said. "I think maybe Fred is all right, but you always get a little more action out of him if you prod him a little. You stepped in right nice there."

"Part of that was just because I felt like prodding," I admitted.

"How'd you like Walt?" he asked, suddenly switching topics on me.

"Seemed okay," I said.

"Like I said, he's the smart one on the force. Figure I'll let him do most of the work on this case. Him and you."

"Suits me," I grunted. "What about this coroner? He sounds like he might get in our hair."

"Ben? Well, Ben's job is mostly a political plum. He's held it for a long time. Except for that, he's retired. He ain't got much to do but sit around and think, so he's apt to come up with a few ideas. Generally we just listen to them and then go on about our business. Once in a while he's got to be pushed one way or the other a little, but"—he chuckled— "Ben pushes kind of easy if you know how to do it."

I lit another cigarette off the old one and tossed the butt through the window. "What do you think about it, Chief?"

"Ain't done much thinking yet," he said. "To be honest, it's because I don't want to. I don't like things like murder in town. We don't have many of them, and I never like them. Even when there's a chance it was done by … a stranger in town, I don't like it."

"I guess I wouldn't either if it were my town," I said. I stared through the windshield to where I could see the hotel. "And I agree with the thinking you haven't done yet. It was either one of the visitors from Hollywood or local talent. Either way, this was strictly an amateur job."

"Why do you say that?" he asked, but he didn't sound surprised.

"The murder, for one thing. Professionals who go in for this kind of stuff don't commit murder unless they have to. In spite of all that broken glass, there wasn't any evidence Enoch put up a struggle. I think he was killed because he knew who was there. Other things point to that, too."

"What other things?"

"I don't know your town," I said, "but I'd guess that in a town this size nobody could do much hanging around without being spotted. If it was a stranger, some nervous old maid would call the cops. But somebody watched around there enough to know that there was always fifteen minutes to half an hour between the time Fred Swanson went for coffee and the time Curtis Hoyt arrived."

"I thought of that," he said, sounding pleased.

"The other thing was the burglar alarms on the cases. They were turned off. A pro wouldn't have known where to turn them off and wouldn't have bothered asking. He would just have clipped the wires and let it go at that. So I think this was somebody who'd been around enough to know where the switch was."

He nodded. "Wouldn't have been hard for anybody who hung around to find out where the switch was. Enoch always did talk a lot." He paused and glanced sideways at me. "Ain't heard you mention any names yet."

"I want a broader look before I mention any names." He nodded and slowed down for the hotel. "You go do your thinking, son, and I'll see you tomorrow."

"Thinking, hell," I said. "If anybody happens to ask you, I'm still angry. I'm going in and see how drunk I can get."

"No law against it," he said, "just as long as you don't start shooting up the town. Drop around in the morning."

"What time?" I asked as he stopped in front of the hotel.

"About ten, I guess."

"I may have to leave my head in the hotel," I said, getting out and giving him a grin, "but I'll be there."

I slammed the door shut and watched him drive off. Then I turned and went into the hotel. I suddenly realized that I hadn't had any dinner; I also realized that I didn't want any except the kind that comes out of a bottle.

The Hocking Hotel had a small bar, with a half dozen booths along one wall. An intimate bar, with the lights low. That was all right with me. I was going to get intimate with some brandy.

There were a couple of men at one end of the bar. I noticed there were some people in two of the booths, but I didn't pay any attention. I went to the other end of the bar, hoping that made it plain enough that I wasn't the social type, and sat down. The bartender came over.

"A double brandy," I said, "and stand by for a refill."

He lifted his eyebrows a fraction of an inch, but that was all. He slid a double glass along the bar, brought up a bottle with the other hand, and poured. He held the bottle and waited.

I tossed it down, letting that first one hit my stomach in a bunch. He filled the glass again and I drank that one.

"Now," I said, feeling the fire starting to kindle in my stomach, "we'll start from scratch."

"Double?" he asked.

"Sure," I said. "No point in pouring a boy's drink for a man." I lit a cigarette while he poured again. I started sipping the drink. I like the taste of brandy, but I'd wanted the fast ones to give me the base for some action.

"Worked up a thirst," the bartender said. He put the bottle down, but he left it on the top of the bar. He'd guessed that I meant business.

"A small one," I said.

"You're that insurance detective, aren't you?" he asked.

"What is it?" I said. "Do strangers smell different here or something?"

"No, sir," he said. He smiled. "It was the double brandy. The dining-room waitress got one this morning and said it was for the insurance detective. We don't get many calls for double brandies, so I made a guess."

"Makes you a brandy detective," I said.

He leaned a little closer and made a pretense of wiping up an imaginary stain on the bar. "I reckon you just came from the murder, didn't you?"

Any other time I guess it would have amused me; now it only seemed to annoy me. I said, "Does everybody in this town know everything as soon as it happens?"

"Almost," he said. "The way I knew about the murder was the phone operator. She heard you get the call."

"That's what I like," I said. "Nice, friendly operators who don't miss a word of your phone calls. It always comes in handy if you forget something that was said."

He ignored my attitude. "They arrest anybody yet?" he asked.

"No," I said carefully. "The Chief and I talked it over and we decided not to do any arresting until the murderer had a chance to get a few more."

This time he got the idea and moved off down the bar. That left me the way I wanted it. Alone. I worked away on the brandy. I had a couple more refills, but the bartender didn't make any attempt to pick up the conversation from where I'd flung it.

That brandy was the best thing I'd encountered in Athens. I was getting a nice glow, but I had to admit it wasn't improving my mood much. I still felt like slugging somebody.

My nose got the first hint that there was a change in the environment. It was the kind of perfume that reached out and started tugging at you before you knew what had happened. Even the brandy fumes had to retreat before it. I turned to see what had brought it in.

I should have guessed. It was the blonde. The darling of the screen. Miss Niki Holden. She was wearing a scarlet evening gown and she looked every inch the movie queen. And there weren't many inches that you couldn't see. I don't know how she had gotten into that gown, but it looked like a deep breath would take her right out of it. She had taken over the stool next to mine.

"Thank God you came in, Milo," she said.

"Somebody was about to attack you?" I asked politely.

"I don't know that I'd want to be rescued from that," she said. "What the hell happens in this town? They roll up the street at ten o'clock. Where does everybody go?"

"Probably home to bed," I said.

She laughed. "So, up to a point, I'm willing to do as the Romans do," she said.

"Athens was a Greek town," I pointed out.

She glanced at me from beneath long eyelashes. "I'm not so sure I go for *that*. Buy me a drink."

I managed to catch the bartender's eye, which had been focused on her plunging neckline, and he came over. She had a scotch and I had another brandy. The bartender wanted to linger—I gather the view was good from where he was standing—but I didn't encourage it and he went back to the long view.

"So what did I rescue you from?" I asked.

"That," she said, pointing over her shoulder. "I was sitting in one of those booths with Gilbert Ireland and some gushing, simpering college girl."

"I wouldn't think a college girl would be any competition for you."

"She isn't," she said, laughing. "But if she'd brought along her brother, he would've been too much competition for both of us."

"The things you say about America's heart throb," I murmured. "Well, why did you stay? It's a big town, at least seven thousand big."

"What the hell would I do?" she said. "Go to a knitting party? Or maybe just walk along the street to be whistled at by college boys or leered at by the old men who sit around the courthouse?"

"They're men," I said.

"Maybe from your viewpoint. I like a man who's old enough to know what he's doing, but young enough to do it."

"I guess you've got a point," I said. I grinned at her. "You're pretty sharp."

"Damn right," she agreed. She gulped her drink. "I wish we were back in Hollywood. Why the hell they make me trek here to look at the natives, or why they even cast me in this coonskin opera, I'll never know. Can you imagine me coming out here in the wilderness and giving birth to the nation?"

"No," I said, "but I can imagine you going through the motions."

She laughed. "You're pretty sharp yourself."

"Sure," I said. "I'm so damn sharp I wasn't able to get out of this town before they nabbed me, and now I'm stuck?"

"There really was a murder?" she asked. "I know that Curtis phoned Laslo about it, but I thought maybe it was just another of his lousy scripts."

"There was a murder," I said.

"How thrilling. You must tell me all about it." She leaned forward and squinted at the bottle on the bar. "What are you drinking?"

"You're looking at it."

"What a shame," she said, looking at me. "I have a bottle of imported brandy in my room. I believe it's twenty years old. But I never drink brandy. Would you like some?"

I finished my drink and didn't even admit to myself that I was feeling reckless.

"Why not?" I said.

I called the bartender over and paid him. Then Niki and I left the bar. I followed her to the elevators. I could understand why men followed her around. The view was so nice from back there.

Her room was on the same floor as mine. I shouldn't say room. It was three rooms and they'd tried to make it look like a suite, but it was still only three rooms.

To my surprise she really had a bottle of brandy. And it was twenty years old. She poured me a drink of it and got herself a hooker of scotch.

"To going through the motions," she said.

The brandy was good. Not only in taste, but it managed to start a separate fire all of its own in spite of the other brandies I'd had before.

I put my glass down and looked at her. She was standing a few feet away from me, staring at me.

"You wanted to hear about the murder," I said experimentally.

"To hell with the murders," she said huskily.

We came together in the middle of the room. This was no soft, yielding woman, melting into the arms of a man. She burned with a hard, bright flame, and there was as much violence in her as I felt within myself.

I'd been right about the dress she was wearing; a deep breath was about all that was needed to get her out of it.

Later I walked across the room to the bottle of twenty-year-old brandy. It still tasted good, but it didn't make me feel much better. I picked my clothes up from the floor and put them on. I took another drink of the brandy and finally I looked at her.

She was stretched out across the bed, the light from the bed lamp making her short-cropped blond hair look like a tarnished halo. Her body gleamed like pale ivory.

"I was right," she said lazily.

"About what?" I asked.

"You're quite a man," she said.

"You're quite a ... too," I said.

She frowned. "Quite a what?" she asked.

"That will go down in literary annals as March's Unfinished Sentence," I said evenly. "I'm not quite sure what you are. Certainly not a woman. You've got all the motions down pat, but the role is a little too much for you. When the lines aren't written on the prompt card, you can't ad-lib. So we'll have to leave it like this: you're quite a."

Her face lost some of its beauty and her mouth wrestled with a word. I beat her to it. I opened the door and stepped out into the hall, closing it behind me. The sound that followed me through the door was half scream.

I went down the hall to my own room. I looked into the next room and saw that Ernesto was asleep. I took a long, hot shower, but it didn't help much.

I knew what had happened, all right, but the knowledge didn't make me feel any better. All evening the anger had been seething in me; I'd been stopped from going back to Denver and I'd felt like slugging somebody. So I had finally slugged the only person who wasn't responsible and couldn't fight back—Greta. I wanted to call her up and explain it to her, but I knew that would only be slugging her again.

Finally, I fell asleep.

FOUR

I didn't feel much better when I woke up the next morning. But I understood what had happened and that the hurt was my own. You can't strike at somebody you love without hitting yourself. At least I was drained of anger and I'd have to handle the residue of guilt better than I had the rage.

Ernesto was up when I looked in his room. It was nine o'clock, so I guessed he'd been up for some time. He seemed to have recovered from his sullenness of the night before.

"Qué hay?" he asked eagerly.

While I shaved and dressed, I told him what had happened.

"Caray!" he exclaimed when I had finished. "Is it not better, Don Milo, to be doing men's work like this than to be hanging around the skirts of some woman? What is it that we do now?"

"It is that we have breakfast," I said. "Then I have to go see the Chief of Police. I don't think it's a good idea for you to come along then, but maybe you can get in on the act later."

He looked a little disappointed, but took it in his stride. "I will be of much help to you, Don Milo," he said. "Even more when I have learned to talk the English. Was I not of great aid in Madrid?"

"You were," I said, which was true. I didn't know how to tell him that this was a different situation and I doubted if he could be of any help, so I didn't try. "Let's go eat."

That was the magic word, making him temporarily forget even the excitement of murder. We went downstairs. A Western Union money order for a thousand dollars was there from the insurance company. I put it in my pocket and we went into the dining room.

There were a number of people there, but I was pleased to see that the Hollywood crowd was absent. We had no more than ordered when Curtis Hoyt appeared. He caught sight of us and came over.

He said good morning, in both English and Spanish, and sat down without asking if I minded. I did, but I let it go.

"How come you're up so early?" I asked. Out of deference to Ernesto, I used Spanish. "I thought you worked half the night and slept out the day."

"Usually I don't get up until about eleven," he said, "but there are a lot of things I want to do today. Anything happen after you left last night?"

"No." I waited until he'd given the waitress his order. "What's going to keep you so busy today? Solving the case for us?"

"Not exactly," he said. "I was only needling the Chief last night when I said that. But what I'm going to do could lead to the solution of the case. Naturally, if it should, I'm not interested in the credit. I'll give it to you."

"That's sweet of you," I said dryly. "And if my investigation happens to turn up a movie script, I'll give the credit to you."

He was impervious to my irony. "I liked the way you handled that special cop last night. Only, to make it really dramatic, you should have reached over and slapped him. That would have made him back down quick."

"It also might have made him flip his lid enough to pull his gun and shoot me," I said. "What's this busy-bee routine, if you're not going to solve the murder?"

"Some loose ends on the story," he said. "You know, this trip here and what happened last night is going to be the best thing that ever happened to me."

"I'm sure Enoch's spirit will be glad to know he did not die in vain," I murmured.

"Don't pull the bleeding-hearts routine on me," he said. "Enoch was a nice old guy and I'm sorry he got knocked off, but not so sorry that it's going to keep me from cashing in on the fact."

"What are you going to do—slip over to the morgue and cut little slices off of Enoch to sell as souvenirs in the Brown Derby?"

"Very funny," he said. "You should stick to the private-eye routine and stop trying to make like a Milton Berle. You haven't got the moxie, kid."

"Oh, hell," I said, "there are times when I think Hollywood's taken over the country. I can't even come out to the sticks without getting involved in swapping glib banter with some guy who's a refugee from Abe Lastfogel."*

He grinned at me. "You're a hep character," he said, "but if you don't like the patter, why don't you go out and see some of the farmers around here? Maybe they'd pay you for shoveling it."

---

* Abe Lastfogel was a talent agent who represented huge stars such as Marilyn Monroe and Elvis Presley, and who was a longtime president of the William Morris Agency.

"Don't look now, but I think you just dropped a couple of consonants," I said. I threw up my hands. "In the meantime, I give up. Just slip your typewriter back in its holster and tell me how Enoch's death is going to make a big man out of you."

"Qué dijó?" Ernesto asked. The last few exchanges between Hoyt and me had been too much for the Spanish language and we'd slipped back into English.

"Your patron," Hoyt explained, "was giving me a little audition of his talents."

"El sastre del Hollywood, que cosía de balde y ponía el hilo," I said, indicating the writer. "The Hollywood tailor who threaded his needle and stitched for nothing."

"Wait until you see what I've stitched," he said. "Dead or alive, Enoch was the answer to my prayers. Before we came here, I'd just finished the third revision on the script of *West to the Hocking.* It was a pretty damn good script then, even if I do say so myself. But then Enoch produced that diary. The script is going to be filled with yellow pages, but it's going to be one of the best damned screenplays that's ever burned up a typewriter. I'll bet you it gets an Oscar."

"Yellow pages?" I asked.

"Yeah. When revised pages are mimeographed, each revision is a different color. Yellow is used for the fourth."

"How far along are you with this revision?" I asked.

"Almost finished. It's been a big job, and Laslo has been griping to beat hell, but he's going to fall on my neck when he reads it. I'm telling you, it's terrific."

"Nice of you to say so," I murmured. "You going to give a screen credit to Enoch?"

"I ought to give one to Mary Hanna," he said, grinning. "But you know what Enoch's murder has done for me?"

"Made you glad it was him instead of you," I guessed.

"I'm going to get an original out of it," he said. He was so excited he was forgetting to eat. "I sketched it out last night after I got back to the hotel. It's going to be a sensational story, and I'm telling you right now, it'll be good for another Oscar. I've even got a title for it: *As Old as Cain*. Good, eh?"

"Colossal," I said. "The only trouble is, I still don't know what the story's about."

"It's about the murder of a guy like Enoch in a small town like this. What else?"

"Seems to me it's been done before."

"Not the way I'll do it," he declared. "As a matter of fact, I've got an idea that my solution for the story is the one for the real murder, too. But I'm going to do a little research today on the story. What are you going to do, Milo?"

I shrugged. "I don't know exactly. I have to go over to the Chief's office pretty soon. Beyond that I don't know."

"Ernesto going with you?"

"Not to the Chief's. Maybe I'll let him tag along later."

"Why not let him come with me?" Hoyt asked.

I could see that Ernesto liked the suggestion. Apparently Hoyt had taken to the kid. It was a good solution.

I knew that on this case Ernesto was apt to merely get in my way, but I didn't want to hurt his feelings by keeping him out altogether. This could solve it.

"Okay," I said. I looked at my watch. "We've just got time to do a little shopping first. You can come along with us."

We finished our coffee quickly and left the hotel. We went first to Western Union where I turned the money order into cash, then found a men's and boys' store. I bought myself a suit—the one I was wearing was going to get a little battered if this kept up—and some accessories. I bought Ernesto some clothes, including, at his insistence, a cowboy outfit. On the way back to the hotel I bought us a couple of bags to carry the extra clothes in. Then I sent Ernesto into the hotel to change. Hoyt went with him, and I took off for the police station.

Chief McArdle was in his office when I arrived.

"How's the head?" he asked as I came in.

"It's still with me," I said. I dropped into a chair beside his desk. "Got everything wrapped up this morning?"

"Nope," he said. "Walt's been doing a little work. He's found Enoch's and Fred's fingerprints all over most everything. He's going to take the prints of everybody else who's had a reason to be down there, but he don't expect it to mean much."

"The case of too many fingerprints."

"Something like that. He says he's sure that the murderer wore gloves. He's also gone over the pictures he took and he's already been over to look at the body again. He figures that Enoch and the murderer were standing in that room and Enoch got it when he turned his back to the murderer."

I nodded. That had been easy to figure from the way the body had fallen.

"Walt got that list from the girl at the hotel," the Chief went on. "According to it, six things were taken—the diary, the silver shilling, the silver bowl, the two books you mentioned last night, and one more." He glanced down at his desk. "A book called *The Countess of Pembroke's Arcadia.*"

"I don't remember the exact value," I said, "but that was one of the valuable ones."

"It adds up to a nice hunk of change," he said, "except for one thing. You think that diary was worth a lot of money?"

"The man who appraised the stuff didn't. I'd guess he was right unless someone proved otherwise."

"Then why in tarnation did the murderer take it?"

"I've got only one guess," I said, "and that might be wrong. Apparently Curtis Hoyt is the only one who's really read it, and he's pretty secretive about what's in it. This could mean that it's filled with some pretty spicy stuff. Maybe the murderer merely wanted to read it."

"Could be, I reckon," the Chief said. "I figure that this list is probably right, but we're going to check up on it anyway. At least on part of it."

"How?"

"The two ladies who own all the stuff except the books. I asked them to come in this morning, and they ought to be here pretty soon."

"They would be … ?"

"Miss Malvyna Hanna and Mrs. Captola Singer. You might say that they're First Family of Athens. I expect this'll be the first time they ever stuck a foot inside a police station."

"How come they had all the old Hanna stuff?" I asked.

"Inherited it. Both of them are descended from old Hiram Hanna. Mrs. Singer came down in a straight line from Hiram and his first wife, and Miss Hanna did the same from Hiram and his second wife. Makes them cousins or something, I guess."

"They didn't know any of this stuff they had was valuable?" I asked curiously.

"Maybe they did, maybe they didn't," he said. "I don't suppose they would have acted any different either way. They're both pretty strong on family. Mrs. Singer was president of the local Daughters of the American Revolution last year; Miss Hanna is this year. Miss Hanna was a delegate to the national convention and Mrs. Singer is on the state board of directors. You might say they're kind of rivals to see which one can make the biggest thing out of the family stuff. I don't think they would part with any of that stuff. I hear that they didn't agree to let that picture company do a picture about old Hiram until they were pretty sure what was going to be said about him. And the only reason they loaned those family heirlooms to the company was because they feel the picture will show everybody how important they are."

I didn't personally know the type, but I'd heard of it. "Who's digging them out of the mothballs so they can come down here?"

He grinned. "I guess they're really pretty nice folks if you get to know them," he said. "I also got Fred Swanson coming in this morning."

"Why?"

"Figured it wouldn't hurt to talk to him again. Maybe after he's had a chance to sleep on it, he'll remember something that will do us some good. If somebody was hanging around to make sure what time he left and Hoyt came in every night,

Fred should've noticed something. On a hunting trip he's usually the first one to spot a squirrel."

I didn't think squirrel spotting was going to do us much good, but I didn't say so. "What else is on the schedule?"

"Ben's going to hold an inquest this afternoon. After that, I'm just going to turn you and Walt loose on it and go back to my knitting. You been doing any thinking on this?"

"Not much," I admitted. "I did do a little this morning, but I can't say that I came up with anything that would make Sherlock Holmes worry about his position. I don't suppose you have any known criminals around town?"

"A few petty thieves and such," he said. "Don't figure any of them would have nerve enough to do a thing like this."

I nodded. "Barring a dark horse," I said, "I'd say that it works down to a list of possibilities something like this. One: Maybe Enoch had some idea of lifting the whole works and planned it with a friend. Only, at the last minute, the friend decided to grab what he could on his own and leave Enoch behind. A variation of this might be that Enoch did too much innocent talking to a friend of his."

"The last might be a possibility. Enoch was a great hand at talking."

"Two," I said, "Fred Swanson. He could have done it himself before he went for the coffee. It would have been easy to hide the loot and go ahead for the coffee to make himself look good. Or Fred could have had a friend who did it while he was out establishing an alibi."

The Chief nodded. "I forgot to say that Walt checked with the waitress at the restaurant this morning. She says that Fred was there from about seven-thirty to ten after eight. But he could've done it like you say."

"Three: Our friend Curtis Hoyt could have gotten there a little earlier than he says. He certainly knew about what time Fred went for coffee and could have been waiting. Then he would have had the fifteen or twenty minutes to kill Enoch and hide the stuff he took. Maybe he had even longer, since we don't know what time he made his first phone call."

"I checked on that," the Chief said, and my opinion of him went still higher. "He made the call to Hollywood at five minutes to eight."

I nodded. "Four: The university professor. Not for the reasons your coroner said, but he must be considered at this stage. He was around enough to be familiar with everything, and Enoch would have let him in if he came around late."

"I think you're right about that," the Chief said. "I know the professor and I can't see him murdering anybody—but then the trouble is, I can't see anybody else doing it either. But we'd better keep him on the list until we're sure. That all?"

"Not quite," I said. "Until we know that they couldn't have, number five is Miss Malvyna Hanna, and number six is Mrs. Captola Singer. And we have to keep our minds open to the possibility that there might be a number seven we know nothing about at the moment."

"I'm not arguing with you," he said, "but how do you figure Miss Hanna and Mrs. Singer? It don't figure that people would steal something that already belongs to them."

"Sometimes it does," I said. "Suppose you owned, say, a silver bowl made by Paul Revere. You'd like to get the money it's worth but you don't want to part with it. You get it insured, then you steal it from yourself and collect the full value from the insurance company. Now you've got the bowl and the money."

He thought about it a minute. "I guess," he said finally. "That blow that killed Enoch was a pretty hard one. Don't seem likely that a woman could hit that hard."

"Normally, no. But you take a woman who's mad or frightened, and she can hit a lot harder than you'd think."

"I guess they belong on the list," he said, but he wasn't very happy about it.

"Something else to keep in mind," I told him. "It looks like the thing was done for money, but we can't say positively. There might be some other motive, and the things were stolen to make it look like a straight robbery."

"I reckon if it was Fred or some friend of Enoch's, it was for money."

"Probably. I imagine they'd follow a pretty straight line."

"What about that writer or the professor?" he asked.

"There we might get on another motive," I said. "I don't know about the professor, but Hoyt makes a lot of money. But, offhand, I can think of another motive that might fit either one of them. I'd say they're both pretty complicated people and on the intellectual side. They were both interested in that diary. Hoyt wouldn't let anybody else look at it, and the professor has been going into a fast decline because he couldn't look at it. If either one of them jumped his trolley a little over that diary, he might kill in order to own it. In that case, the other things would be taken as a cover-up."

He looked at me in astonishment. "Why would anybody steal a diary like that if it ain't worth anything?"

"Maybe one of them fell in love with it. If that was true, I'd say most likely Hoyt, since he's the only one who's had a chance to study it."

"Fall in love with it?" he said. He shook his head. "You sure you ain't trying to make fun of a small-town cop, son?"

"Not me," I said. "You ever hear of Queen Nefertiti, Chief?"

He shook his head.

"She was an Egyptian broad who lived several thousand years ago," I said. "She was a real ball of fire from all accounts. Anyway, several years ago there was a statue of her in a Berlin museum. And some guy fell in love with the statue and stole it from the museum so he could look at it all the time."

"Beats me," the Chief said. He grinned. "This is the first time I ever heard of a guy getting hot around the collar over a statue or a book."

"It takes all kinds," I said. "Suppose Hoyt has been reading this diary, as we know he has. It was written by a woman back in eighteen hundred and something. Maybe she was a pretty hot number in spite of all the petticoats they wore in those days. Maybe this comes through in the writing. If he's off his rocker a little—and who isn't?—maybe he starts thinking of her as being real. In that case, he might steal the diary in order to keep her with him. I don't say it was that way—I'm only saying that it could be."

The door opened and the young cop of the night before stuck his head in. He saw me and grinned. "Hello, Mr. March," he said.

"The name's Milo," I told him. "We're supposed to work together if there's ever anything to work on, so let's not be so formal."

"Okay," he said. His gaze shifted to the Chief. "Fred Swanson's here. So are Miss Hanna and Mrs. Singer."

"Show the ladies in," the Chief said. He didn't sound too eager. "I guess maybe I'd better talk to them, but when they leave, you bring Fred in."

"Right." He disappeared and the door closed.

A moment later the door opened again and two women came sailing into the office. Sailing was the only way to describe it. The one in front was a little on the plump side and she was wearing a dress that looked as if it might have been handed down from some of her ancestors, too. It was shiny black, and the only color on it was a brooch fastened at the high collar. She looked about fifty, but her face was smooth and bland except for the few thin lines that had been made by frowning and pursing her lips. She was doing both things as she came in. The other woman was as skinny as the first one was plump. She was dressed a little more fashionably, but she didn't look like an ad for Hattie Carnegie. She seemed about the same age, but her face was lined to indicate that she worried with her whole face. Her mouth was set in the same grim way as Miss Hanna's—as if they'd both been eating something they didn't like. Both of them wore their hair pulled tightly back and gathered in an uncompromising bun at the back. The skinny one wore rimless glasses that pinched the bridge of her nose. They looked like a couple of portraits that Grant Wood might have done on a bad day.

"Chief McArdle," the first woman said grimly, "what are you doing about recovering my possessions?" There was a sense of power in her voice, an awareness that her words would be obeyed, which was not lessened by the nasal quality.

"Land's sake, Malvyna," the second woman said, "it just happened. Give the man a chance." Her voice was shrill and whining, filled with eternal complaint.

"You keep out of this, Captola Singer. After all, it wasn't *your* things that were taken."

"Ladies," the Chief said calmly. "We're doing everything we can, Miss Hanna. This gentleman here is Mr. March, from the insurance company. Mr. March, this is Miss Hanna and Mrs. Singer."

They both looked at me suspiciously and said "How do you do" as though with one voice. Then they turned their attention back to the Chief, dismissing me.

"I demand to know what you are doing about this situation, John McArdle," Miss Hanna said. "Things have come to a pretty pass when a body's property isn't safe. What were you doing, I'd like to know, to just let anybody march in and make off with my possessions?"

"There was also a murder," the Chief said mildly.

Her mouth drew tighter. "That Enoch Drake," she said. "He was bound to come to no good end. I haven't slept a night since he was given that job. I just knew he'd steal everything or something."

"He drank," Mrs. Singer said. Her tone made it clear that this explained everything.

The Chief glanced at me and tried again. "Lots of men drink without ever getting murdered," he said. "Now, ladies—"

"Not without deserving it," snapped Miss Hanna. "Not that I mean to speak ill of the dead. Under the circumstances, I suppose, I should go to his funeral—it's only my Christian duty. But he wasn't a fit person to take care of our family heirlooms."

"The Hand of Providence," Mrs. Singer said, "is evident or everything would have been taken. But something must be done. Land's sake, a body just isn't safe in her own bed."

Lady, I thought, you'd be safe in anybody's bed.

"I asked you ladies to stop in," the Chief said hurriedly before they could get started again, "because I thought you might give me a little help. We have a list here of everything that was in the house on Lancaster Street, but we're not positive that it's complete. We've checked off the things that are missing. I wonder if you ladies would look at the list and see if there's anything been left off it." He held out several sheets of paper.

Miss Hanna took the sheets, and the two of them bent over them, looking as if they might suddenly attack the typewritten words. They read through the list without a word, then Miss Hanna replaced it on the desk.

"Everything is there," Miss Hanna said. "On the list, I mean. But my silver bowl and my silver shilling are gone no matter how many lists you make up."

"Nothing of yours missing, is there, Mrs. Singer?" the Chief asked.

"No."

"If you ask me, there's something pretty strange about *that,*" Miss Hanna said. She looked at the skinny woman. "Don't you agree that it is, Captola?"

"I do not," snapped Mrs. Singer. "My poker was used to kill that poor Enoch Drake. Land's sake, that's even worse than if they stole it."

"I can't imagine why anybody'd *want* to steal an old poker."

"I want to thank you ladies for coming down here," the Chief said. Obviously, he was trying to get rid of them now. "It was a big help and we appreciate it."

I could see that they weren't going to let it go at that, so I decided to give him an assist. "You can be sure," I said, "that the Great Northern Insurance Company will do everything it can to assist Chief McArdle. I think we may have your things back very soon."

The two women turned to examine me as though aware of my existence for the first time.

"Well, how about that," said Miss Hanna.

I was about to answer her when I realized it was an exclamation, not a question.

"Mr. March, isn't it?" Miss Hanna said. "Are you any relation to the March family in Pomeroy?"

"I don't think so," I said. "I'm from Denver, Colorado."

"Denver? Oh, we have a lovely chapter there."

"Chapter?" I said.

"The Daughters of the American Revolution," Miss Hanna said. She fixed a firm eye on me. "The one organization that's doing the most about Americanism today. Don't you agree, Mr. March?"

I'd had about all of this I could stand. "I've always thought the name was unfortunate," I said solemnly. "Revolution, you know. The Smith Act. I've always thought it would have been much better if we'd had a McCarran Subversive Activities Act back in those early days to keep out the riffraff that came over on the *Mayflower*.* The Indians should have thought of that."

They didn't quite know what to make of that, so they both merely drew their breath in sharply. It sounded a little like a hiss.

"And that General Washington," I said. I dropped my voice to a stage whisper. "He drank, you know."

That settled it for them. As though operated by a single string, the two heads swiveled back to the Chief.

"We," said Miss Hanna, her voice coming up out of a deep freeze, "will expect some results, Chief McArdle." They turned and started to sweep from the room. I let them sweep as far as the door.

"Just one more thing, ladies," I said. They stopped and turned, fixing their gazes somewhere in between the Chief and me. That was probably meant to show me that I was just beyond the pale. "I would like to know where both of you were last night between seven-thirty and eight."

They both looked at the Chief as though expecting him to turn and destroy me. The Chief wasn't happy about the situation, but he was smart enough to be busily looking at something on his desk. When they couldn't get his attention,

---

* The Smith Act was the Alien Registration Act of 1940, designed to prosecute immigrants who advocated the overthrow of the U.S. government. The McCarran Act of 1950 was aimed at monitoring subversive organizations and keeping Communists out of the U.S.

the two women went back to looking at a spot somewhere in between us.

"Well, I never!" Mrs. Singer said.

"Does this mean," Miss Hanna asked, "that you believe it necessary to question us about the theft of my property?" She was determined to consider the murder as being of secondary importance.

"I just like to know where everybody was," I said cheerfully. I decided to drive another barb in while I was at it. "Of course, if you don't feel like answering, you can always fall back on the Fifth Amendment."

Her lips tightened. "I cannot speak for others," she said pointedly, "but I was on my way to visit Mrs. Stout. She was a very good friend of my mother's and she is now bedridden, so I try to cheer her up as much as I can. I believe I arrived at a quarter past eight."

"Where does this Mrs. Stout live?"

"On North Congress Street."

"How far is that from Lancaster Street?"

"I believe it is about three blocks," she said grimly.

"Anybody see you while you were on your way there?"

"I'm sure I couldn't say. I didn't, however, skulk through the back streets, so it's very possible."

"Mrs. Singer," I said.

She tried to make another appeal to the Chief with her eyes, but it met with no more success than the others. Her voice had even more of a whine to it when she answered. "I was at home, sewing, until Mr. Singer arrived."

"At what time was that?"

"Eight-thirty, I believe."

"You were alone?"

"Yes." Her thin lips closed sharply over the word almost before it was out of her mouth. "Our union has not been blessed by any children, so I was alone."

That, I thought, was a blessing for the children who might have been born to her.

"Where is your home?" I asked.

"On Mound Street."

"How near is that to Lancaster Street?"

"One block," she snapped.

"Thank you, ladies," I said gravely. "If I were you, I wouldn't worry about the fact that neither one of you has an alibi. I've usually discovered that murderers try to fix an alibi for their time."

They both gave what in Victorian times would have been called a gasp but was nearer to a snort, then wheeled and departed.

The Chief pulled out a handkerchief and mopped his brow. "You know," he said, "I'd rather have to deal with a whole pack of desperate criminals than talk to those two women." He glanced at me and there was a twinkle in his eyes. "You were a little rough on them, son."

"Not half as rough as I would have liked to be," I said. "Did you notice that that charming chunk of femininity, Miss Hanna, implied that she couldn't be sure that the other one hadn't swiped the family valuables?"

"I noticed," he said. "Don't think it means anything except that Miss Hanna is a contrary woman. Her and Mrs. Singer are kind of rivals, like I told you, and they're apt to be a little spiteful to each other."

"And Mr. Singer didn't get home until eight-thirty," I said. "Can't say I blame him—but maybe we ought to add him to our list until we know where he was."

"Not him," the Chief said. "Sam Singer wouldn't blow his nose unless his wife told him to."

The door opened and Walt Sawyer looked in. "Ready for us, Chief?" he asked.

"I reckon," the Chief said, sighing.

The young cop threw the door wider and Fred Swanson came into the room. Walt followed him in and closed the door.

Swanson was wearing a baggy tweed suit instead of the uniform he'd had on the night before, but otherwise he looked much the same. Big and burly, with the same lack of expression on his face. Yet it seemed to me that there was something different about him. I couldn't put my finger on what it was, but I sensed it.

"Hi, Chief," he said. He looked at me, his gaze neither friendly nor unfriendly. "Hello, March. You wanted to see me, Chief?"

"Yeah," the Chief said. "Nothing very important. I thought maybe you'd remembered something since last night."

"What would there be to remember? I told you everything I knew about it. Too bad about Enoch, but that's the risks about taking a job like that." He sounded more aggressive than he had the night before.

The Chief caught it, too. I could tell by the way he cocked

his head to one side and looked at Swanson. "Yeah," he said. "Still, what with you being in something of a spot with it happening when you was supposed to be on duty, I thought maybe you'd do a little heavy thinking last night."

"I ain't in no spot," Swanson said. "I didn't have nothing to do with it."

"Didn't say you did. Reckon at the best, though, you'll lose your job with the movie company."

He made a suggestion about what they could do with the job. "I've been thinking," he said. "Maybe I'll quit the job anyway. I don't cotton much to them Hollywood people and the way they been treating me. I think I'll quit this afternoon."

Walt Sawyer leaned forward and I could see he was feeling it, too. "Got another job, Fred?" he asked.

"Nope."

"You weren't also thinking of leaving town, were you?" the young cop asked.

"Why would I leave town?" Swanson asked. "But I don't have to keep the job just because I'm staying in town. No law that says I have to keep a job if I don't want it."

"We're going to get some funny ideas about anybody who leaves town in the next few days," I said.

His gaze swung back and forth between the three of us. It reminded me of a bull looking at the matadors.

"I don't like the way you're talking to me," he said. His tone was half anger and half whine. "I ain't done nothing and you got no right to sound like I had. You keep talking like that and I'll have the law on you even if you are cops. A man's got rights."

"Of course, he has, Fred," the Chief said soothingly. "We wasn't aiming to say that you did anything. Just figured that a man like you, what's had police experience, is more apt to see things than somebody else. Thought maybe you'd remember noticing somebody hanging around one of the nights when you went for coffee."

"Already told you I didn't. If you ask me, maybe it was some guy that's been mad at Enoch for a long time and finally got enough likker under his belt to do something about it."

"And what about the things that were stolen?" Walt asked.

"Maybe the guy only noticed them after he killed Enoch and decided to grab whatever was easy to carry."

"Pretty smart grabbing," Walt said dryly. "Except for the diary, he grabbed the most valuable things in the room."

"Well, that's the way I figure it," Fred said. "Enoch used to be out on Sugar Creek twenty years ago. Maybe it's somebody from then and they just waited until now."

"Never knew anybody on Sugar Creek to be that patient," the Chief said. "But we'll keep it in mind, Fred. If you do happen to remember anything, you'll tell us, huh?"

"Sure."

"Guess that's all, then, Fred. Thanks for stopping by."

"Glad to help you if I can, Chief," he said. He looked at me and snickered. "Figure you'll need all the help you can get, what with one of them insurance dicks under your feet. You let me know there's anything I can do."

"We'll do that, Fred," the Chief said solemnly.

The three of us watched silently while the big man ambled from the office.

"Something funny going on there," the Chief said when the door closed behind him. "Last night Fred was kind of scared of losing that job, and today he's going to quit."

"Yeah," Walt said. "He's feeling a lot more sure of himself." He looked at me. "You suppose maybe Fred did it and last night he was scared because he didn't have the stuff hidden too good? By today he would have had a chance to do a good job of hiding, so he'd feel pretty cocky about it."

"Maybe," I said. "Offhand, I'll admit I'm a little thrown by the people in this. Most of the cases I'm on, you can be a little more certain of the motives. My first guess about this Fred is that he'd be a guy who'd steal cash if he had a chance, but he wouldn't be apt to steal something like a book even if he knew it was valuable. But I could be wrong."

"You're probably right," the Chief said slowly. "I never knew anything against Fred except that he was kind of shiftless, so I never thought of him being crooked. But now that I think of it, I got an idea you about hit it."

"So what's made him change?" Walt asked.

"I can think of one thing," I said. "Maybe he did remember something from last night or from the past week and decided that blackmail was an easier way to make a living than working. He wouldn't be the first to arrive at that conclusion."

The two cops exchanged glances. "Never thought of Athens as being much of a place for blackmail," the Chief said. "Never had any here that I know of."

"A Hollywood writer would make enough to pay healthy blackmail," I said. "Maybe even a university professor does. I don't know. On the other hand, maybe Fred doesn't need a lot to make him happy, so that almost anybody could meet the bill."

"I think we'd better keep an eye on Fred," Walt said.

"A good idea," I said. "I don't suppose you can do much here about shadowing someone, can you?"

They both grinned. "Pretty hard in Athens," Walt said. "On the other hand, we can fix it so that it'll be hard for Fred to leave town or start spending any money without us knowing about it. We can't tail him, but we can have half the town help us watch him."

"I guess that's an advantage," I said. "What was this business he pulled about Sugar Creek?"

"Oh, that," the Chief said. "There's a little mining town a few miles out of town called Sugar Creek. During Prohibition most of the bootleggers were up there. Practically every house was a bootleg joint. Enoch Drake had a beer joint up there. That was about his only law-breaking, and everybody was doing it then. Fred's idea sounded like just talk to me. How about you, Walt?"

"I don't remember Sugar Creek's prime," the young cop said with a grin, "but I think Fred was just making noise "

The Chief looked at his watch and grunted. "Wasted the whole morning on Fred and them women."

The young cop grinned again. "They were sure breathing fire when they came out of the office," he said "What happened?"

"Milo wanted to know if they had alibis for the murder."

The young cop laughed.

"Might as well have some lunch," the Chief said. "Then it'll be time for the inquest. After that you two can take over the case and not bother me with it till it's solved, Want to have lunch with us, Milo?"

I nodded and the three of us left.

We had lunch in a little restaurant not far from the police station. Our talk, while we ate, nibbled around the edges of the case, but that was all. We still didn't have enough even to talk about. We'd gotten far enough to be suspicious of Fred Swanson, but not far enough to take the suspicion off the others. Unless something happened to give us a break, it was just going to be hard work, slogging along and trying to break down the time element to point at one more than the others. I didn't like the looks of it.

"I don't suppose," I asked them, "that you have any rare-book collectors in town, do you?"

"None that I know of," the Chief said.

"Got a few who go for the works of Fanny Hill, but that's about all," Walt said.*

"They're all over," I said, grinning. "If money was the motive, I guess they'll have to hit someplace big. Columbus or Cleveland, or farther away."

"I talked to the B and O** and the bus station," the Chief said. "Anybody starts leaving town that way, we'll know about it."

"They wouldn't have to leave town," I said. "They could just pack up the stuff and mail it to a dealer. If they did,

---

* A reference to the fictional heroine of *Fanny Hill* by John Cleland, a scandalous English novel, written in the eighteenth century but still considered obscene the 1950s, available only in illicit editions.
** The Baltimore and Ohio Railroad.

there'd be no reason for the dealer to suspect it wasn't legitimate."

"Didn't think of that," the Chief said. "Walt, you might stop around at the post office this afternoon and ask them to keep an eye out for suspicious packages."

"It's a bitch," I said. "I guess we can't go around just grilling everybody in town."

"There'd be hell to pay," Walt agreed. "Only person I'd like to grill is that blond movie star at the hotel."

I looked at him. There was an expression in his eyes I recognized. I suspected it had been in the eyes of half the men in town since Niki Holden had showed up.

"I'd be the last one to say anything about a lady," I said solemnly, "but I expect she wouldn't put up much of a fight."

"You sound like you knew," he said with a grin.

"I'm just a guy on a delayed honeymoon. I wouldn't know anything for sure. Except that I'd like to get this case solved and get the hell out of town."

"Reckon we could pull everybody in for questioning," the Chief said. "Guess nobody'd raise much of a fuss about Fred and the Hollywood writer. But I got the feeling that if I started questioning the professor and them two women, the whole town would be buzzing around my ears."

"I expect so," I said. "No, there isn't much to do but wait and keep checking over the time. Walt, you're going to check on Dr. Rheames sometime today? About where he was last night?"

The young cop nodded.

"I'd like to get a map of the town, too," I said. "Is it possible?"

The Chief nodded. "You can get that at the Athens Board of Trade. Nine East Washington Street. I'll walk you over after the inquest. Got something in mind?"

"Just want to check," I said. I looked at the young cop. "When you check with the professor, find out where he lives. You can call me at the hotel."

He nodded.

We finished lunch talking about other things. The Chief gave me a rundown on the advantages of living in Athens, including a description of Zaleski State Forest, Lake Hope, the Hocking Caves, Burr Oak Lake, and the local gun club. When he finally ran down, the young cop took over. He wanted to know all about insurance detection, and I kept him entertained until we'd finished.

We went over to the courthouse for the inquest. There wasn't much to it. The Coroner testified, and the only other witnesses were Fred Swanson and Curtis Hoyt. Ernesto was there, watching all of it and understanding none of it. He cheerfully thumbed his nose at me but didn't come over to me, so I gathered he was enjoying himself with Hoyt.

The verdict was the expected. Enoch Drake had met death at the hands of a person or persons unknown. The rest was up to us.

Leaving the courthouse, we split up. Walt Sawyer took off in one direction and the Chief and I went in another. We stopped in at the Board of Trade. He introduced me to a couple of people and got me the map of Athens.

On the way back to the hotel, I picked up a bottle of brandy. Then I went up to my room, steering wide of the bar. I had a hunch that was where Niki would be, and I didn't feel like wading through her passes.

Upstairs I put in a call to Greta. I wasn't able to be very optimistic about when I'd get back, but it made me feel a little better just to talk to her. After I hung up, I got a bellboy to bring me some paper and I got down to work.

First, I marked up the map, putting in the location of the hotel and of the Crescent Museum. I marked in the approximate spot where Mrs. Singer lived and the spot where Miss Hanna visited. I could only make it approximate since I didn't have their exact addresses. After that, I started making my little list.

The phone rang. It was Walt Sawyer. He had just finished talking to Dr. Rheames. The professor had been out taking a walk the night before from about a quarter past seven until eight-thirty. He always took a walk in the evening. He didn't think anybody had seen him.

"I don't think he's really involved," Walt said then. "He deplored the death of one of our citizens, but he was really upset about the loss of the diary. I don't think he's that good an actor, so it probably means he didn't have anything to do with it."

"I don't seriously suspect him," I said, "but we also can't eliminate anybody until we've got more than we have now. Where's he live?"

"North Congress Street."

"Okay," I said. "I'm going to be here at the hotel. Call me if you get anything—especially on our friend Fred."

"Right," he said cheerfully.

I hung up and made another mark on my map, right near where I had the one for Miss Hanna. I went back to work on my list.

An hour or so later I had the list finished. I poured myself another drink of brandy and stretched out on the bed to study it. It looked like this:

Curtis Hoyt:

Hocking Hotel. Left the hotel at 7:30 (according to Ernesto) for the museum on Lancaster Street. Should be no more than a 10-minute walk, but according to Hoyt he didn't arrive until 7:45 or 7:50. His first phone call was made at 7:55, so it may have been even later. He could have had at least 5 or 10 minutes. Probably enough. The murder couldn't have taken more than 2 or 3 minutes. Five minutes should have been plenty of time to hide the stolen articles—outside or upstairs? He would have known Fred's usual time for going after coffee and there would have been no trouble about Enoch letting him in.

Motive: Possible compulsion to own the diary. A weak motive, but possible. (Could money be a motive with him? Makes a lot of money, but could be in debt.) If not this, question: Why is he so secretive about the diary?

Fred Swanson:

Has alibi for the time. Confirmed. But he could have engineered it and gotten a friend to do it. Certainly knew the schedule and the location of the burglar alarms. Friend could have gotten in by telling Enoch he had a message from Fred.

Two other possibilities: (1) Someone could have wanted to pull the job and bribed Fred to be absent. And Fred intends to use the information to blackmail the person. (2) After the murder, Fred remembered seeing someone around the last few days, or remembered seeing someone around as he left last night, and is blackmailing that person or intends to.

Motive: Nothing but money here. Direct and simple.

Positive: Fred knows something or thinks he does.

Enoch Drake:

May have planned it with a friend, and then was double-crossed by the friend. Would fit all the requirements. He knew the schedule and location of burglar alarms. Check his friends.

Motive: Money from sale of other antiques, insurance money for his books. But, with either Enoch or Fred, why take the diary, which wasn't worth anything?

Dr. Thurman Rheames:

Lived within 5- or 10-minute walk of the museum. No alibi from 7:15 to 8:30. If he was in the habit of walking around the town every night, nobody would pay much attention or be apt to remember seeing him. As invisible as the post-man. Earlier he was unduly disturbed at not being permitted to see the diary, but this could be put down to scholarly impatience. In his favor is fact that he was upset about the diary's being missing. Could be acting.

Motive: Can't rule out money, but certainly must put it secondary. First place goes to diary. Why? Doubtful that scholarly interest could lead to this murder. If he did it, the reason must be close to the one assigned to Hoyt: Nefertiti.

Malvyna Hanna:

Claims she was on her way to North Congress Street, only 5–10 minutes away. She could have detoured. Looks strong enough, both in character and muscle, to have done the killing. The same thing applies to her as to Rheames. She says she often walked to visit woman on Congress; she might be a familiar-enough sight so no one would pay any attention to her.

Motive: This one might be a little more complicated. Maybe she needs money. (Ask McA. if he can check this.) Being the type she is, she might not want to sell anything because that would tip off others that she needed money. This way she could collect insurance money and no one would have to know she needed it. But there might be other motives. What? Hard to say. She looks like a repressed, frustrated person— might get any kind of a bee in her bonnet. Even might imagine that Enoch wasn't treating her stuff right (identification of self with possessions?) and the stealing was to cover up.

Captola Singer:

Lives only 5-minute walk from museum. Was alone until 8:30 so had plenty of time to go there and back. Same reasoning applies to her as to M.H. Same type of personality. It's written all over her face. People with that much frustration and that much repressed hostility capable of anything under right circumstances.

Motive: No money motive here since none of her things taken. Could be hostility aimed at M.H. Or maybe some complicated reason I can't even guess yet. Could fact that her poker was used in the killing mean anything? Instinctive grabbing of something familiar? (On other hand, if M.H., she could have used it to throw suspicion on C.S., as she did in conversation.)

All of these, excepting Enoch, had the time and could have had the motive. It is reasonable to assume that Enoch would have readily admitted any one of them to the house. They were all, in some degree, parties in interest to the exhibition. Undoubtedly they were all around enough previously to have learned how to turn off the alarms.

John Doe:
If there is a John Doe, it might take forever to find him. But, since the local newspaper carried a full story on the value of the exhibit, there might be a John Doe, and he might be any one of the 7,000–8,000 people in Athens. McA. says there are no real criminals in town, but a petty criminal might have seen this as his chance to graduate; or this might be the one crime of an otherwise honest person. How gain entrance? John Doe could be someone who was known to Enoch and was let in on the basis of that. John Doe might have been someone Enoch didn't know but who offered a good-enough story so that Enoch let him in. Probably wouldn't have been hard. John Doe might also be Jane Doe—a woman that Enoch was mixed up with. If one of

these is the answer, this case could drag on forever. Our best chance is if Fred Swanson is blackmailing the murderer and will lead us to him or her.

Well, that was my list. I lay on the bed and stared at it until my eyes were popping out, but I still didn't have a favorite. The only thing I was sure about was that Fred Swanson knew something and maybe he'd provide the break.

Walt called once to see how I was doing. I told him. He agreed that Fred was the only candidate he had for anything, too.

"It has to be blackmail," I said. "I can't see him pulling the job, but he must have found some sort of gold mine from the way he was acting today, and that must be it."

"You think he's already collecting?" Walt asked.

I thought about it. "No," I said. "I could be wrong, but with this town knowing everybody's business, my bet is that he'd make the contact pretty carefully."

"We'll try to keep track of him," he said. "Anything else you want to suggest?"

"Not now," I told him. "I want to do a little more thinking and then sleep on it. Maybe tomorrow I'll have some ideas."

"See you then," he said and hung up.

Ernesto came in about five, full of good cheer. *"Oye, tú,"* he exclaimed. *"Qué hay?"*

I gave him a quick recital of what had happened, including what I thought about the case. I left out only one thing and that was the fact that Curtis Hoyt was on the list. I could see that Ernesto was pretty fond of the writer, and there was no point in making him feel bad unless it was necessary.

"So what do you think, *chico?*" I asked when I'd finished.

He screwed up his face, thinking about it. "*Yo caigo en ello,*" he said finally. "It is one of the two women who did it."

"Why do you say so?"

"Whenever there is trouble," he said, shrugging his thin shoulders, "it is always a woman that causes it."

"You're taking in a lot of territory, *chico,*" I said, grinning at him. "I'll admit that these two women are lacking the more feminine qualities, but I've known some who were fine."

"*Consejo de mujer vale poco,*" he said scornfully.

I laughed. "You're only quoting half of the proverb," I said. "It goes, 'A woman's advice is of little worth, and he who won't take it is a fool.' … So, what did you and your friend do today?"

"We walked around and talked to people," he said. He'd strutted over to the bathroom door and was admiring himself in the full-length mirror. He was wearing the cowboy suit I'd bought him.

"What did you talk about?" I asked.

"Don Curtis said he was getting to know some of the people for his story for the cinema."

"That's all?" I asked in some surprise. I'd thought from the way Hoyt had talked that he was going to do something that was connected to the case.

Ernesto shrugged. "It is what he said. I could not understand the language. He said we were going to do it tomorrow also."

"He didn't go to see anyone in particular?" I asked. I watched Ernesto carefully. I knew he was quite capable of giving me a cover-up story if Hoyt asked him to.

"Only some professor at the university. Don Curtis said he was very learned man who knew all about the history of this town. But he didn't look so bright to me. *Pedazo de alcornoque.*"

"I don't think he's a blockhead," I said. "What did Hoyt want to see him for?"

"Some foolishness about the history of this town. I hope that I will not have to learn the history when I go to this school you mention." He went through the motions of a draw from the hip.

"You will," I said. "Learn any new English today?"

"You bet," he said in English. "Hi Ho, Silver—They went thataway—Seven come eleven, baby needs a new pair of shoes."

I laughed. "I'm not so sure that this Hollywood writer is a good influence on you."

"He says perhaps I could go into the cinema and make much money."

"You will go to school and make much learning," I said firmly. "Hungry?"

"Don Milo, you know I am always hungry," he said truthfully. *"Qué diablos!* I never thought there was so much food in the world as there is in this America."

"Let's go eat, then," I said.

I made him go and wash his hands and face, a chore he looked upon with something akin to horror, then we went downstairs. Calling myself a coward, I stayed away from the dining room. We went out and found a restaurant. After we'd eaten, I took Ernesto to a Western movie. Keeping my voice low, I translated as much of it as I could for him. By the time the movie was over, we were pals again.

On the way back I picked up a couple of paperback mystery novels and some comic books. Remembering that I had a bottle of brandy for myself, I got some candy for Ernesto. Then we went straight up to the room. I sent Ernesto into his room with the comic books and the candy and told him to be sure to go to bed early. I got into bed with a glass of brandy and one of the mystery novels.

First I called Greta. While I was talking to her, I tried pretending I was back in Denver and we merely had twin beds, but it was too much even for my imagination. Finally, I hung up and started working on the brandy and the mystery novel.

Somewhere along about the time the hard-boiled private eye was slugging his fourth villain with one hand while he made a pass at his fifth wench with the other, I fell asleep.

The bell jangled in my ears and wouldn't go away. I rolled over and reached for the alarm clock. All I could feel was a glass. Finally I opened my eyes and looked around. I realized that I was in a hotel room in Athens, Ohio, and there was no alarm clock. But the bell was still ringing.

By the time I'd figured out that it was the telephone, Ernesto had padded in from the next room and picked up the receiver.

"*Diga?*" he said.

I looked at my watch. I'd thought it was no more than midnight, but it was almost eight o'clock.

Ernesto was listening with the air of bewilderment, but finally light dawned on his face. "*Un momento,*" he said.

He turned to me. "It is someone mentioning your name, Don Milo."

I took the receiver and mumbled into it.

"Milo," said a voice. It sounded excited. "This is Walt Sawyer."

"Walt?" I said. "What the hell is this? You been up all night?"

"Almost," he said soberly. "I thought you might like to know that Fred Swanson made his contact."

"Did you pull him in?" I asked. I looked at my watch again and groaned. "It's inhuman to arrest anybody this early in the morning."

"I didn't arrest him," he said. "He's dead."

It took a minute for it to soak in. When it did, I was wide awake.

"Murdered?" I asked.

"That's my idea," he said. "But the Coroner thinks otherwise and the Chief ain't sure. Get down here."

"Where?"

"Mulberry Street." He gave me the address. "Hurry up."

I put the receiver down and jumped out of bed, grabbing my clothes.

"*Qué hay?*" Ernesto asked.

"I'm not sure," I said, "but I think Athens is about to learn the facts of life—the hard way."

FIVE

I felt that I was being yanked out of bed in the middle of the night, but when I got out on the street it looked like the whole town had been up for hours. I walked the one block to the taxi stand and got a cab to take me down to Mulberry Street.

The cab pulled to a stop in front of a small, weatherbeaten house. I paid him off and went up and knocked on the door. It was opened a minute later by Walt Sawyer.

"Boy, am I glad to see you," he said. "I'll tell you all about this later. Come in and look around and see if you don't agree with me. The Chief will listen to you. He's still a little afraid that I'm showing off."

He led the way into a small room just off the hall. It was dark and smelly in there. The air was pungent with smoke, but in addition to that, it smelled as if it hadn't been aired in weeks. My eyes adjusted to the gloom and the room swam into focus.

The Chief of Police was standing to one side, listening to the Coroner—the guy who looked more like he ought to be an undertaker. He stopped talking as I came into the room.

"Hello, Milo," the Chief said. "Sorry to drag you out of bed so early, but Walt thought you ought to look this over before we moved the body. You remember Ben?"

I did. Ben remembered me, too, but he didn't look too happy about it. Or maybe that was just his professional air.

The first thing I saw was the body sprawled face down on the floor. It was Fred Swanson, still wearing the tweed suit, but he looked smaller in death than he had in life. His head was lying near an open fireplace. There had been a fire in it, but it was now out except for a little smoke still spiraling up from it. I could see a few charred pieces of paper among the ashes. As I drew closer, the smell of stale whiskey was added to the other smells in the room.

There was a large bloodstain on the frayed rug near his head. He'd been dead long enough for the blood to dry and turn brown.

I glanced around the room. The furniture was as battered as the rug. It looked like a room that had seen a lot of living, most of it on the careless side. Then I caught sight of the table near where the Chief stood.

There was a bottle of whiskey on it, with maybe an inch still left in it. But that wasn't what caught my eye. Next to it was a large silver bowl. A silver coin was beside it. And next to that, neatly piled one on top of another, were three books. I glanced at the Chief.

"Yeah," he said, nodding. "It looks like we caught our thief and murderer, but too late."

"What do you think happened?" I asked.

"I know how Walt here feels," the Chief said. "He probably talked to you. But I guess it's pretty clear. Fred did a little too much celebrating last night—you can see by the bottle how much he had. We know that he only bought the bottle last night. Anyway, he apparently got more than he could handle and sometime during the night he stumbled and fell. He hit his head against one of them andirons and it killed him."

I looked down at the body again. This time I saw the andiron right beside his head. Even from where I stood, I could see the smear of dried blood on it.

"No doubt about it," the Coroner said importantly. He might have been talking to me, but he was looking at the Chief. "The position of the body, the wound, the position of the andiron—it all points to accidental death. Clear-cut."

"It can't be," Walt Sawyer said. "I'm telling you that he had a visitor last night."

"Nobody's denying that," the Chief said gently. "You know, I'd go along with you, Walt, if there was anything to show you're right. But a man having a visitor don't mean he was murdered. We'll try to find this visitor—likely whoever it was will come forward when the news gets out—but it'll probably only help establish Fred's condition."

"No doubt it's an accident," the Coroner repeated firmly.

"The thing that knocks your murder theory into a cocked hat, Walt, is the stolen stuff," the Chief said. He was talking to Walt, but looking at me. "If you was right that Fred was killed because he found out who stole all that stuff, then it wouldn't all be here. Anybody desperate enough to kill two people just wouldn't go and dump all the stuff like this. It don't make sense. Now, does it?"

"I still say he was murdered," Walt said stubbornly.

I didn't know why Walt was insisting that this was murder. I still hadn't seen anything that would indicate anything else but an accident. Maybe he only had a hunch. I hated to admit it, but I was feeling the same way. There wasn't anything I could put my finger on, but I felt there was the smell of murder in that room. The logical answer to that was that the room stank and that was it, but I wasn't ready for that kind of logic. Maybe, with me, it wasn't any more than the fact that I knew both the Coroner and the Chief wanted it to be the way they'd described it. They weren't used to this kind of thing in Athens, and they wanted it to be over and done with. Closed. Maybe they didn't even know that was what they wanted, but it was.

"What about the diary?" I asked.

"It's here, too," the Chief said. He reached around on the table and produced it. "Fred was either carrying it around or reading it when he fell and it went into the fire. It got burned a little around the edges, but that's all."

"All the lights were turned off when I broke in this morning," Walt said. "You mean he was reading it in the dark?"

"Then he was carrying it," the Chief said.

"Let me see it," I said. I held out my hand and the Chief gave it to me. The cover was a little charred and I could see some of the leaves were brown and curling. I held it in my hand and let it fall open. This diary had been growing in my mind in connection with the first murder and the robbery, and I felt a little nameless thrill as I opened it. Except for the curling of the edges of the pages, it didn't seem harmed by the fire. The writing on the page that was open was a little faded, but still easy to read. The writing of Mary Hanna, done a hundred and fifty years earlier. She wrote in what was probably called a neat hand in those days. Each letter was perfectly formed, the strokes even and unhurried.

I glanced over the page in front of me and read how Mary Hanna had seen an Indian skulking around the back of the house. She had gotten the children inside and stood at the window with a rifle until her husband came home. Some woman. I couldn't help comparing her with Niki Holden, who was going to play her in the movie. Some casting, I thought.

I thumbed idly through the book.

"You see," the Chief said, and it sounded to me as if he were almost pleading, "it can't be anything but accidental death, Milo. No thief would come down here, bringing his loot, kill Fred, and leave everything for us. It's all right out here to be seen. Fred was the murderer and thief, but he didn't live to enjoy it. It's all solved and cleaned up. You've got the property all back, and now you can go ahead on that honeymoon of yours."

I wanted to go on that honeymoon more than I wanted anything else, but suddenly I knew I wasn't going to go on it just yet. I knew it even before I knew why. Something in that diary set off an inaudible bell. I had to thumb through several more pages before I found what it was.

I looked around the room. There was a calendar hanging on the wall. I went over and tore off a sheet and went to the fireplace. I bent down and slid it under one of the black wisps of burned paper. Carefully. I lifted it up and looked at it. Outlined against the thin ash, I could see two or three well-formed letters. Then there was a faint stirring of air from somewhere and it fell apart. I straightened up and faced the Chief. He was watching me anxiously. So was the Coroner, weaving his bony fingers together.

"Sorry, Chief," I said. "Walt is right. It's murder." The Chief let his breath out in a long sigh.

"Impossible," the Coroner said explosively. "Look at the situation. Look at the body, the way it's lying. The bottle on the table, the andiron, the—what makes you say that?" His voice had progressively lost its force and turned querulous.

"Look," I said, holding out the diary and slowly riffling the pages. "There are at least twelve or fifteen pages that have been torn out of this diary and burned in the fireplace. A man who's going to have an accident and drop a book in a fireplace doesn't first tear out the pages that he wants to be sure get burned."

"You're sure about that?" the Chief asked. He stepped closer and examined one of the torn pages in the book. Then he glanced at the fireplace. "How can you be sure that those are the pages? Maybe they were torn out before."

"It's impossible," the Coroner muttered.

"The one I picked up," I said. "I could see the writing on it before it fell apart. There are four or five more pages in there yet which are still holding together although they're burned. But we can be sure." I turned to Walt. "Do you have the equipment to salvage those?"

"No," he said. "I know a little of how it's done, but I don't have the equipment to do it with."

"Then there's only one thing to do," I said. "Put a screen in front of the fireplace, or we can tape newspapers over the front of it, so that the pieces won't blow apart. Also, try not to cause any breezes while taking the body out. And send for an expert to come down from Columbus. He'll be able to fish those pieces out and photograph them so that they can be identified."

The Chief looked a little doubtful.

"The insurance company will pay for it," I said. "I know your budget isn't very big."

"Why will they pay for it?" he asked. "Everything's been recovered."

"I know," I said. "But even when there's full recovery, insurance companies don't like to have the criminal get away. If he's caught, it helps to discourage others."

The Chief nodded. "All right, I'll do it."

"But what will I do?" the Coroner asked. "Maybe you're right about them pieces of paper—then again maybe Fred tore those pages out and burned them himself. It ain't enough for me to bring in a verdict of murder. Don't like the idea of another murder, anyway."

"I don't either, Ben," the Chief said. "Soon as we announce there's been two murders in two days and the murderer ain't caught, half the town's going to go into a panic."

"That's easy," I said. "The Coroner doesn't have to hold the inquest immediately, does he?"

"No."

"So hold the inquest off for two or three days. It shouldn't take more than two days for us to get an expert down here and get his report. In the meantime you can let the accidental-death theory go around. Just don't tell anyone it's murder.

It may even help us if the murderer thinks his plan has been successful."

"Sounds good to me," the Chief said. "How about it, Ben?"

"Only one trouble," the Coroner said. "Down at the paper they're going to think it funny I don't hold an inquest right away. I don't usually put them off that way."

"You can think of something to tell them," I said. "Say you want to go fishing or something. You can think up some excuse."

"I suppose so," the Coroner said glumly.

"And make sure that this room and this house are sealed up until after the expert gets through," I said. I looked at Walt. "You got me up before breakfast this morning. Can we go somewhere and get a cup of coffee while you tell me how you happened to find this?"

"I could use one myself," he said. "Okay, Chief?"

"Yeah," the Chief said. "Ben and I can handle everything, I guess."

"Make it look good," I said. "You can tell them anything along the line I suggested and say it's a quote from me. Come on, Walt."

He and I left, leaving the Chief and the Coroner staring unhappily at the body on the floor.

"Thanks," he said as we climbed into his car.

"It should go the other way," I told him. "If you hadn't called and been suspicious, I might have accepted the obvious. In fact, I might have wanted to accept it as badly as they did."

"Don't get the Chief wrong," he said. "He wouldn't cover anything up. He just wanted everything cleared up so badly, he began to see what he wanted to see."

"I know," I said. "With the circumstances just a little bit different, I might have done the same thing. After all, I don't want to hang around here."

"You don't have to now, do you?" he asked, pulling in to the curb in front of a small restaurant.

"Technically, I suppose I don't," I said slowly. "But if you don't mind, I think I'll see it through."

"Glad to have you," he said, and obviously meant it.

"I'm not sure why," I said. I was thinking out loud more than explaining to him. "I was sore as hell at getting stuck here, and I still want to get back to Denver as quickly as I can. But there's something about this case … I want to see it cleaned up—and fast."

"I think I know what you mean," he said as we got out of the car. "It's this business with Fred. If you can speak about a murderer being normal, I suppose it's normal for one to kill again when he's threatened with blackmail. But there's something creepy about a person committing one murder in order to steal stuff worth several thousand dollars and then to give it all up at the time of the second murder. It looks to me like somebody's flipped his lid but good."

I was thinking he was probably right as we went into the restaurant. There was just enough wrong with this case to make it look like the work of a psychotic. And if that was true, we could very likely toss all our motives out the window. The murderer might not even have any motive except a whim, or the motive might come out of something entirely imagined and therefore almost impossible to guess.

Inside the restaurant I suddenly thought of something.

There was a pay phone on the wall. I used it to call the hotel and asked them to ring my room. Ernesto answered and I told him to go down to the dining room and I'd give them orders to give him breakfast. I asked him if he wanted to wait for me to come back to the hotel. He said he'd promised Hoyt to go with him again. So I told him to have fun, then I jiggled the hook until I got the operator back. She connected me with the dining room and I told them what to give Ernesto and to put it on my bill. Then I hung up and went to join Walt. He was sitting in a booth at the rear of the restaurant.

As I sat down opposite him, I noticed for the first time that he looked tired. There were dark circles under his eyes and the eyes were slightly bloodshot.

"You look like you've been up all night," I said.

"I damn near was," he said. He broke off as the counterman came over and we ordered breakfast. He waited until the man had shuffled away and then continued. "You started it." He grinned.

"Me?"

"Yeah. After I talked to you yesterday, I got to thinking about what you said—that Fred would probably try to contact the murderer so as not to be seen. I had an idea about that. Athens doesn't have much night life, so it seemed to me to make sense that they'd probably meet late at night. After I got off duty last night, I started kind of drifting around town until I located Fred. Without him getting the idea, I managed to keep a pretty close watch on him. He had supper uptown, then played pool for a while. Finally, just about dark, he quit and started home. On the way he stopped and bought that bottle of whiskey. Then he went straight home. I parked up the street and settled down to wait for him to either leave again or go to bed."

"Why didn't you call me?" I asked. "I could have come out and helped."

"Now I know I should have," he said. He was embarrassed. "But at the time I thought I could handle it. As you'll see in a minute, if I hadn't tried to be such a big shot, everything might be all wrapped up now."

"Don't beat yourself over the head," I said. "There isn't a guy in this business who hasn't sometime or other tried to be a hero. What happened?"

"When Fred went into the house," he said, "he went into that room where he was found this morning. You probably noticed that the room is in the front of the house. As soon as he entered the room and turned on the light, he pulled the blind. But Fred was obviously pretty nervous and kept walking around the room. I could see his shadow each time he passed the window. A couple of times I could see him drinking. The fact that he was so nervous made me even more certain that your hunch was right."

"What time was this?"

"About nine o'clock. I sat there in my car and Fred paced back and forth in the room. I began to think that was all that was going to happen, but Fred didn't show any signs of going to bed, so I stuck with it. Nothing happened until almost three o'clock. By that time I'd been staring at the window so long I almost missed it. But suddenly there were two shadows thrown against the blind. Fred had a visitor."

"Man or woman?"

"I couldn't tell. They weren't standing near the window, so the shadows were a little on the lumpy side. The visitor had obviously come in the back way, and that was when I wished that I had called you. It just hadn't occurred to me that this would happen. I thought of still calling you, but quickly realized that the visitor might leave while I was trying to find a phone—I'd have to come uptown to get a phone at that time of night. So I did the best thing I could do. First I got out of the car and went up close to the window, hoping I could hear them talking, but I couldn't hear anything. Then I walked down to the corner where I could still see the front of the house and also see down Van Vorhes Street. That didn't let me see the rear door, but I could see one street by which a visitor might leave. But from that position I could no longer see any shadows against the blind—or it may be that they didn't get near the window again."

"How long was the visitor there?"

"I don't know," he admitted. "Obviously the visitor left by the back door and then cut off in the opposite direction from Van Vorhes. I didn't see anyone or hear anything. But about three-thirty, the light was turned out. Now I can guess that Fred was dead then and it was the murderer who turned out the light and left. But at the time I thought the visitor had left and Fred had turned out the light himself. I really slipped on that one."

"It can't be helped," I said.

"I waited another half hour," Walt said, "and when the light didn't go back on and Fred didn't come out, I thought he'd gone to bed. It was then four o'clock. I went home and went to bed myself, setting my clock for six-thirty this morning. I was back here by a little after seven. My idea was to hang around and see what Fred did this morning, if anything. But luckily I happened to walk around back to look at the house. The rear door was wide open. I investigated, with the results you know. But I certainly loused this one up. I'm sorry, Milo."

I waited until the counterman served our orders and went away. "Maybe you did and maybe you didn't," I said. "Unless you had caught the murderer red-handed, it's possible you still wouldn't have had too much of a case. We can't tell now, but it may work out even better this way. You didn't see or hear anything that would give you any kind of clue to the visitor?"

"Nothing," he said. "I might add that as I went home, I cruised around some, hoping that I'd catch sight of someone who might be the visitor. I had no luck on that, either."

"Incidentally," I said, "what about the investigation back there now?"

"The Chief and I talked about that while we were waiting for you," he said. "We agreed that I should be free to work with you, providing you agreed with my feeling about it. There is another man in the department who can use the camera and the fingerprinting material. We called him and he was already on his way down with the equipment when you were there."

"How come?" I asked.

He looked uncomfortable. "It was my idea," he said. "I was pretty sure you'd agree with me that Fred was murdered. I thought you might want to start moving fast, and I wanted to be able to go with you—not because I thought it necessary for someone to be with you, but because I wanted to be in on it."

I laughed. "You've been reading too many mystery novels," I said. "You're right in saying that I want to move fast, but it carries an implication that I know which way to move. I don't. So I'm a man in a hurry but without any destination."

He laughed.

"I've got a list of possibilities," I said, "now reduced by one, or a fraction of one. That list consisted of Curtis Hoyt; Enoch Drake, if he was double-crossed by an accomplice; Fred Swanson, who may have been double-crossed by an accomplice; Dr. Thurman Rheames; Malvyna Hanna; and Captola Singer. As a seventh possibility I have added a John Doe, who might be any one of the other citizens of Athens. With the exception of Enoch, none of the specific individuals had alibis covering the first murder and robbery. I doubt if any of them will have any better alibis for last night."

"I doubt if anybody has an alibi for three o'clock in the morning," he said, grinning. "Or if they do have, it'll be one they'll be reluctant to mention."

"Probably," I agreed. "I've been doing a little off-the-cuff thinking while we were coming over here. It seems to me that I may have to revise my approach to the list. Originally, although I admitted the possibility of other motives, I gave first consideration to money. After this murder of Fred and the return—or discovery—of everything, I think we'll have to think more about other motives."

"Such as?"

"I'll be damned if I know. At the moment, I have only two thoughts about it. One is that the murderer's motivation, in regard to the theft and final disposal of the objects, must be based on neurotic, and possibly psychotic, reasons. The second thing is that the diary plays the most important part in the whole picture."

"I wondered if you were going to get around to that," he said. "If the murderer of Fred carefully tore out certain pages and burned them, doesn't it indicate that those pages might hold the story to the motive?"

"Maybe. If we don't find out before, we may know more about that in a couple of days after the expert has been here. We'll be able to save some of the pages. But it's also very possible that those pages have furnished only an imagined reason. I can't think of any good logical reason why the diary of events of a hundred and fifty years ago should lead to murder.

"Something else on this point. Going back to the night before last. If Enoch was murdered in order to get the diary, it would seem to follow that the other things were stolen in order to conceal the real reason. In other words, to make it look like gain was the reason."

"Looks that way," he said.

"After going to all that trouble," I said, "why throw it all away twenty-four hours later by leaving everything in Fred's room and attempting to burn the diary?"

He looked puzzled. "It looked to me like the murderer wanted to make it look like Fred had committed the theft and the first murder."

"Yes," I said, "but why? There was nothing pinpointing this on any person, so the murderer was still safe. And there was nothing to indicate that the diary was especially important. So why abandon a plan which was still good for one which was not necessarily any better?"

"Sounds like a spur-of-the-moment decision to me," he said. "The murderer was threatened with blackmail by Fred, let us suppose. The murderer saw an opportunity to get rid of the threat and at the same time have the case marked as solved."

I nodded. "I thought of that, too. The only trouble with it is that there are two parts to it and they're as different as if two people were involved."

"What do you mean?"

"One," I said, "our murderer learns that one person knows what he did and intends to blackmail. On very short notice he decides to kill the blackmailer. On probably shorter notice he devises a method which looks like accidental death. And a damn good job. Remember that there was nothing about the manner of death which tipped us off. If you hadn't been there last night and if it hadn't been for the diary, I expect we would have accepted the Coroner's theory. Right?"

"Right," he said.

"Now we come to the second part. The murderer might have planted one object, say the silver shilling, on Fred Swanson, and let us conclude that Fred had either sold the other things or hidden them somewhere. If we had accepted the accidental-death setup, I'll bet we would have accepted this. But instead of doing this, he tosses away all the objects he had risked so much to steal. He puts them forever out of his reach. But he does even more than this. He rips pages out of the diary and burns them, leaving evidence that they have been torn, then tosses the whole diary on the fire—when any idiot knows that a closed book will practically never burn up unless you've got a hell of a big fire.

"So he executes a brilliant maneuver and at the same moment he does something so hysterical and stupid that it's hard to believe the same person did both things."

"Maybe," Walt suggested, "that was his unconscious desire to be caught. I've read that a lot of criminals have that."

"They do, but I don't think that's it."

"Then you think there were two people involved?"

I shook my head. "No, I think that this is the proof that we are dealing with an unbalanced person. Oh, he—or she—may seem perfectly normal to most people, but he isn't. I think he has some kind of monomania, or obsession—and if I knew exactly what, I'd know who it was and what the diary meant to him—and that when that obsession is threatened, everything else will go to the winds in an attempt to defend it. It is possible that the complete diary was such a threat, or he thought it was; it's possible that Enoch Drake was such a threat; it is certain that Fred Swanson was such a threat. I think the murderer was then in such a frenzy that he would have thrown over everything else, no matter how carefully planned. In other words, his instinct of self-preservation is all focused on one thing and is oblivious to all other threats."

"You're getting a little deep for me," Walt confessed, "but

I expect you know what you're talking about. I can think of one other reason why he did this."

"What?"

"He may have been frightened by your presence and figured that you'd be out of the case if the insured articles were all returned."

"Flattering, but untrue," I said. "In the first place, I haven't done anything to frighten anybody. If I'd been nosing around, that might be different. You're just being too damn modest."

"Didn't mean it that way," he said, grinning. "I think the Chief and I could solve this case or any one that could be solved, but there might be a lot of people in Athens who don't think we can do more than arrest some drunken college student. All right, Milo, granting that you're right, what's the next step? Go over that list of yours and see who on it might be ripe for a straitjacket?"

"No," I said. "That might be the more sensible way to tackle it, but I'm tired of sitting on my rear end. We've had two murders in something like thirty hours and the only thing we've got now that we didn't have then is a fancy theory. No, first I'm going to take a chance on whittling the list down a little. I say take a chance because all I've got to go on is ... call it a hunch. Willing to go along for the ride?"

"You're the driver," he said.

"Damn it," I said, "you and the Chief are going to spoil me. I'm used to cops getting real tough about anybody snooping around in their territory. I won't be able to get back to normal. ... Well, first, I'm going to throw out the idea that Enoch Drake was mixed up in it in any way with an accomplice. If he had been, I think it would have been for a simple profit motive. What do you think?"

"I'll buy that," he said. "It sounds like Enoch."

"And," I said, "I'm going to clear Fred Swanson of being anything except a blackmailer, and a pretty stupid one at that."

"We still don't have any proof that Fred was blackmailing," he said, "but I think you're right."

"I'm also going to throw out Curtis Hoyt temporarily."

"Why?"

I grinned. "For one thing, I think he's too eccentric to be crazy. Seriously, I told you I have nothing to go on but a hunch, but I can't see him in this. Maybe I'm wrong and we'll have to come back to him."

"Okay. Who else?"

"We'll leave the rest in—Dr. Rheames, Mrs. Singer, Miss Hanna, and John Doe."

"How do we go about finding John Doe?" he asked.

"We might stumble on him," I said. "I want to talk to the other three today, but first I want to kind of float around. I want you to take me around to see people who know any one or all three of them. I want to get a fuller picture of them. Maybe we'll get some things that'll fit in. While we're at it, we might even stumble onto somebody else who fits the bill, and that might be John Doe."

"There's just one problem," Walt said. "It won't be long until the news about Fred is all over town. The way we're letting it go, the impression will be that the case is finished. So why are we asking questions?"

"I still have to write a report," I said, grinning. "We'll lead off with Fred Swanson, with me trying to get a picture of him and his motives, and I'll sneak the others in the back way."

"Sounds all right," he said. "I'm ready whenever you are."

We paid our check and left the restaurant. First I had him drive me back to the hotel. Ernesto had already left with Hoyt. As we went by the bar, I caught a glimpse of Niki Holden. She turned on the frost for me, but I caught a speculative gleam in her eye as she looked at Walt. He saw it too and his chest measurement increased by at least two inches.

"File that look away," I said, "until we're through, and then you can find out what it means."

He laughed. "I know what it means," he said. "The question is, will she change her mind?"

"Her mind isn't the part of her that acts as a guide," I said dryly.

Upstairs I took a fast shower and shave and then slipped into some of the new clothes that I had bought the day before. Then we took off.

It was a busy morning. We saw ten people before we knocked off for lunch. I must say we got all sorts of opinions about the three I was interested in. The ideas about Dr. Rheames ranged from thinking he was a red-hot Communist about to blow up Athens with a vest-pocket-size H-bomb to saying he was a second Aristotle. The opinions on both Mrs. Singer and Miss Hanna ranged from "a great American woman" to the "nosiest witch in town." About the same labels were attached to both, but never by the same person. Most of those who loved Mrs. Singer couldn't stand Miss

Hanna, and the other way around. We also ended up with a list of some thirty local screwballs who had been nominated for the position.

"Looks like we drew a blank there," Walt said as we had lunch.

"Not completely," I said. "I wasn't expecting any miracles. Mostly I wanted to get a more rounded picture of the three persons we're going to see this afternoon. By striking a balance on what I heard, I got it. Does everybody in Athens have such strong opinions about everybody else?"

He laughed. "Probably. This is the first public opinion poll I've ever conducted."

"When this is over," I said, "you can take another poll to see who's the most unpopular visitor Athens ever had."

He laughed again. "Do you find that unusual?"

"Everybody loves the insurance investigator," I said. "Especially if he drops dead."

"Don't be bitter. You could always go in for something else."

"Yeah, something like plumbing. I've had plenty of experience digging around in cesspools." I saw the grin on his face. "You think I'm kidding. What's the biggest case you've worked on since you've been on the force?"

He wrinkled his brow. "I guess maybe a house robbery last month. We caught the guy two days later. I know it isn't much of a crime—"

"I wasn't meaning to belittle you," I said. "I just was pointing out the reason you didn't understand me when I talked about the cesspool. But stick with me on this one, Walt, and I think you'll get the idea."

"Probably," he said. He glanced at his watch. "Shall we pick up our plungers and go to work?"

I grinned at him. "Always leave the tools behind. Then you can go back for them. Let's go. First stop, Dr. Rheames."

We paid the check and left. We parked near the university campus and walked up the shaded brick walk. I'd glimpsed the campus a couple of times before, but this was the first time I'd had a good look at it. I had to admit it was beautiful.

We found the right building, and after asking some student finally found the office of Dr. Rheames. The professor was in, sitting at a desk piled so high with books and papers that all we could see at first was the mop of white hair.

"Be with you in a minute," he said without looking up. Walt and I stood there and waited, and after a couple of minutes he raised his head and looked at us.

"Oh, you're not students, are you?" he said. He stared at us. "It's Walter Sawyer, isn't it? Of the police department." He shifted his gaze to me. "I believe I met you two days ago. Mr. ... March, of the insurance company?"

"That's right," I said. "We'd like to talk to you for a couple of minutes, if we may."

"Certainly," he said. "Pull up two chairs and sit down." He waited until we were sitting beside his desk. "Is it true that the man who was a guard in the museum had an accident and died last night? And that you found all the missing items in his room?"

"That's the way it looks now, Dr. Rheames," I said. "But I have to write a report and I'm around asking a few questions."

He stared at me and his eyes were alive with intelligence.

"I think I understand," he said with a little smile. He evened up the stack of papers on the desk in front of him. "I believe it was yesterday that this young man phoned to ask me where I was the night before between seven-thirty and eight. I told him I was out walking and that I saw no one who could bear me out. I assume from this that I was to some degree suspect at the time. Is that correct?"

"As a matter of fact, yes," I said.

"And am I correct in assuming that you're not completely certain about the crime of last night and that I may still be somewhat in the shadow?"

I decided to play this one by ear instead of the way I'd planned. "Yes," I said.

He smiled. "You honor me," he said. "It is years since anyone has accused me of acting in a passionate manner over anything that has occurred in the present century. I am flattered."

I think he meant it.

"Now you may ask your questions," he said. "When you've finished, I'd like to ask you a question."

"Seems like a fair exchange," I said. "I hadn't originally intended to ask it quite so bluntly, but where were you at about three o'clock this morning?"

"Three o'clock? I'm afraid I can't be of much more help than I was before. I worked at home, on my book, until approximately midnight. Then I went to bed after having a glass of warm milk. I'm afraid that I went to sleep almost immediately and didn't awaken until seven this morning. But, of course, you have only my word for this."

"Are you married?" I asked.

"Yes, I am, but my wife was asleep until only a few minutes before I myself awakened. I'm sure that you have other questions to ask, but I'd like to ask my question now. I'm afraid I'm impatient to know the answer."

"Go ahead."

"Was the diary recovered?"

"Yes."

He smiled. "I doubt that it would hold up in a court of law, but I might also add in my defense that if I had been guilty of that particular crime, I'm sure that I wouldn't have returned the diary until I had the opportunity to study it thoroughly. It would have taken more time than this."

Walt and I both laughed. "On the other hand," I said, "there were several pages torn out of the diary when we recovered it. A man might tear out the pages that interested him and return the rest."

"Pages torn out!" he exclaimed. "Gentlemen, you are accusing me of a crime far more serious than the ones of which you have suspected me."

"Not accusing you," I said. "As a matter of fact, the torn pages were burned. But we think some of them can be saved— that is, that we can get a photographic copy of what the pages held."

"Thank goodness for that," he said. He pulled out a handkerchief and mopped his face. "You gave me quite a start. Do you think I will be permitted to examine the diary once it is no longer needed as evidence?"

"I'm afraid I have nothing to do with it," I told him. "I imagine that pending the disposal of the estate of Enoch Drake, the diary and other books will remain on loan to the motion-picture company. The screenwriter, however, has indicated that he's about through with his rewrite and I imagine it won't be long until you can see it."

He glared at us. "I assure you gentlemen that if I had intended to commit murder, my first victim would have been that young man who writes screenplays. It is a bitter commentary on our times that the needs of a movie come ahead of the recording of history. I suppose I should be used to it. Many of my students seem to be more interested in Gabby Hayes than they are in Rutherford Hayes."

"And the Mona Lisa's been replaced by Lisa Ferraday,"* I said. "Things are tough all over. Tell me, why are you so anxious to see the diary?"

"I thought I had made that obvious. I am writing a local history, which is almost completed. If there is fresh information in the diary, no matter how slight, I'd like to incorporate it in my book."

"What makes you so certain that there is fresh information in it?" I asked.

"It is merely a guess, Mr. March. I confess that Mr. Hoyt's actions have whetted my appetite. But under any circumstances I would want to check any such new source as a matter of course."

"What do you think might be in it?"

"Anything," he said. "Hiram Hanna first came West with

---

* Lisa Ferraday (1921–2004) was a celebrity actress of the 1950s, appearing in such films as *I Was an American Spy.*

Moses Hewit in 1790. They both lived on Blennerhasset Island, the spot that figured in the Burr Conspiracy. Later they both moved to this area. Hanna, in fact, lived right about where Home Street now is, near the Hocking River. He continued to live there through a period important in the growth of Athens. You must remember that this university got its first state charter in 1804 and that Athens County was formed March 1, 1805. I should imagine that, if nothing else, the diary may contain reactions to some of these events. It may have even more important information."

"Such as?"

"Hiram Hanna," he said, "played an important part in the early days of this territory, yet we don't know too much about him. We know that he married his first wife at Blennerhasset around 1793. He brought her up here with him, but then apparently deserted her about 1799. She died in 1800. The only reference to this I have been able to dig up indicates that she may have been killed by Indians. Hiram Hanna then married his second wife in 1801. We don't know the exact date. There is still another mystery about Hiram Hanna which the diary might clear up."

"What's that?"

"Hiram Hanna died in 1807. August sixth, to be exact. We know from another source that Hiram Hanna had two rather violent arguments that day and one major disappointment. He had a fight with an Indian trader and was beaten rather badly. Later he had another fight with an Indian scout named Jamie Welch. Then he went up toward Strouds Run, where he expected to complete a land trade with another settler. For some reason, however, the settler had changed his mind and refused to go through with the trade. Hiram Hanna returned home and committed suicide."

"What do you expect the diary to show on that?" I asked.

"I don't know," he said. "Nothing sensational, I assure you. But Hiram Hanna was a perfect example of the pioneer extrovert. He was a hard drinker and a hard fighter. He also played an important role in the founding of Athens County. It would seem that there was a general disintegration of character, culminating in suicide. His wife's daily notes might shed much light on this and enable me to give a more rounded picture of one of our founding fathers."

"With one foot firmly planted on the brass rail," I said.

"Something like that," he said, smiling. "You must realize that picture would fit many of our founding fathers."

"Very interesting," I said. "I wish I had more time to sit around and discuss it with you. Do you mind, Dr. Rheames, if I ask you a very personal question?"

"No." His eyes were bright with interest.

"I've spent the morning," I said, "talking to various people around Athens. I'll admit that I discussed you and other people with them. This really has nothing to do with the case—that is, I think it doesn't—but I am curious about the variety of opinions concerning you. These ranged from the highest admiration to the thought that you automatically should be considered suspect of murder. I might add there were a number of opinions that you were eccentric. I'd like to hear your explanation of this variety."

He laughed. "All professors are considered eccentric," he

said. "Those who so described me were, I'm sure, merely using a handy cliché to describe me as a nonconformist. As for the rest, it might be chalked up to the times. Being a professor and one who thinks, I am automatically what is today known as an egghead. Parenthetically, I might point out that the term 'egghead' is directly derived from the German word *Eierkopf,* a word very frequently applied to persons like myself by the Nazis.

"Be that as it may, as I have stated, I am a man who attempts to think. Consequently, I have frequently expressed myself on various national and international matters. I am opposed to Communism, but I am also opposed to Fascism, believing that essentially both methods are the same. That is, both stem from a belief that the end justifies the means. Personally, I favor a belief that the means justifies the end. I have spoken out on all these matters, as well as in favor of the United Nations and against the use of atomic and hydrogen bombs. I have also gone on record as approving of our Constitution as written and not as some would have it rewritten. We are now living in such a climate of fear that this is enough to label one a dangerous radical. That, sir, is my position."

"I've had some experience myself in those matters," I said dryly. "I did some work for the State Department a couple of years ago and had to give up Russian dressing for the duration."

He laughed. "I might hasten to add, however," he said, "that I do not consider Athens unique in this matter. I'm sure that I would be regarded in the same light in almost any other locality. It is the times, not the place."

"Well, we could kick this around all day," I said. "Tell me, Dr. Rheames, you seem to have thought about this case some. Got any ideas about it?"

"Under the circumstances," he said with a wry grin, "I suppose I could invoke the Fifth Amendment—or would that lay me open to the charge of being a Fifth Amendment murderer? But seriously, Mr. March, I don't have any very concrete ideas. I know nothing about this latest development. Yesterday I was of the opinion that the crime had been committed primarily to obtain the diary and the theft of the other objects was to make it appear otherwise. It doesn't seem to me that the return of the diary or the destruction of its pages fits in with this hypothesis, so I must have been wrong."

"Did you suspect anybody?" I asked.

He hesitated. "To my shame, sir," he said. "I must confess that my first thought fixed upon Mr. Hoyt."

"Why?"

"I'm heartily ashamed of this whole thing," he said, "for it indicates the sort of reaction I deplore. I realize now that it was a result of my anger. I felt that Mr. Hoyt was unjustly keeping me from seeing the diary and that the robbery was an extension of this."

"You felt you were being persecuted by Hoyt?"

The professor was obviously uncomfortable about this, but he didn't seem to be trying to duck anything. "I must confess that I did. Otherwise, I'm sure that I wouldn't have followed that line of thought."

"And you thought he committed a murder and the theft merely to persecute you more?"

"No, not that far," he said. "I merely meant that that led me into thinking of him."

"What did you think was his motive?"

"I had been trying to find some reason why Mr. Hoyt refused to let me see the diary. Suddenly it seemed to me that the two things were tied together. The diary had been written by a young woman, perhaps a young woman with a vivid personality. It occurred to me that Mr. Hoyt might have become infatuated with her, as he came to know her through her writings—this may sound strange, sir, but there are certain classical precedents. This, I felt at the time, would explain his reluctance to show me the diary and would also explain the crime. I now confess that I was obviously in grievous error."

"You had Nefertiti in mind?"

"You know of the fascinating queen?" he said in some surprise.

"I thought of her in connection with the motive myself," I said. "You've been here at the university long?"

"Seven years. Before that, I was at that suspect institute, Harvard."

"You're obviously a student of Athenian history; I would guess you're equally a student of modern Athens. Do you have any theories you'd like to offer?"

He shook his head. "After that one attempt, seen in the light of sane afterthought, I have given up all attempts to play the role of the amateur detective. I can assure you of that, sir."

"I don't know about Walt and Chief McArdle," I said, "but I don't have any objections to amateurs. There are a few exceptions, but most cops are merely amateurs who get paid for it."

"We don't mind amateurs, either," Walt said. "Wouldn't do us much good to do so. Three-fourths of the town is always telling us how to run the department."

"Okay," I said, getting up. "I guess we've bothered you enough, Dr. Rheames."

He looked surprised again. "No instructions about not leaving town or anything of that sort?"

"Not from me," I said. "That would be up to the cops."

"I've got no such orders," Walt Sawyer said. He grinned at the professor in a friendly fashion. "But the next time I come along when you're going to be asked a simple question, I think I'll bring you a public speaking permit."

The professor laughed. "I'm sorry, young man," he said. "University professors are apt to run off at the mouth. It's an occupational hazard."

"I don't mind listening," I said. "We'll see you around."

"Good day, gentlemen," he said as we left.

We left the building and started down the walk.

"What do you think, Milo?" Walt asked.

"I don't know," I said honestly. "He seemed to talk pretty freely."

"What about the 'persecution' business? That seems to fit in with your ideas about the personality of the murderer, doesn't it?"

"Maybe," I said. "Let's go see Mrs. Singer. Where is it that she lives?"

"Mound Street."

We got in the car and drove off. It was a five-minute drive. Mound Street was a short residential street, lined on either side by good-sized shade trees. The houses were mostly old, but attractive. We stopped in front of a pretty white house surrounded by a white picket fence.

We climbed out of the car and went in through the gate. The yard was small but well landscaped, with plenty of flowers. We walked up to the front door and knocked. There was no answer.

"What do we do now?" Walt asked.

"I don't know," I said. "Think she's apt to be gone all afternoon?"

"No way to know. She and Miss Hanna are both pretty active in the D.A.R. and other local organizations. She might be to a meeting or maybe just running around chewing the fat with someone. I don't suppose there's any reason why she'd have to come home before it's time to get her husband's supper."

"If she has to then," I said. "From the one look I had at her, I'd guess her husband is lucky if she lets him eat. Well, let's wait a while. If she doesn't come, we'll go on and see Miss Hanna and come back later."

Under one of the trees in the front yard, there was a rustic table and bench. We went out and sat there to wait.

An hour went by without any sign of Mrs. Singer. Finally I suggested that we go on to Miss Hanna's.

She lived on Fremont Street, not far away. It was a small yellow bungalow. It looked like an old maid's house, although I couldn't put my finger on anything that gave me the impression. We went through the gate and found ourselves in what seemed like a jungle of roses. I realized that they were planted in a planned fashion, but everywhere I looked there were roses. The air was heavily cloying with the scent.

Again we drew a blank. There was no answer to our knock. Once more we decided to wait. It was already after four o'clock; if we had to spend much more time waiting, the afternoon would be shot. There was a rose arbor near the front of the house. We sat there.

"Suppose they both left town on the lam?" I asked.

He laughed. "I can't imagine either of them running very fast. What happens if she doesn't return pretty soon? Should we come back tomorrow, or would you rather have them come in to the station?"

"No, I'd rather talk to them at home," I said. "If you don't have a date, we'll just keep shuttling back and forth until one of them shows. I don't want to wait until tomorrow."

I chain-smoked as we waited. The cigarette smoke helped to offset the smell of the roses.

Malvyna Hanna arrived about a half hour later. The gate opened and she bustled through. She was just plump enough to be panting a little from the efforts of walking. She was wearing another shiny black dress. An old-fashioned black hat perched precariously on her head. In one hand she carried a black bag, almost as large as a suitcase, with a drawstring top.

She was almost to the front door before she saw us. She stopped and peered at us. She sniffed audibly when she recognized me.

"Walter Sawyer," she said, "what are you doing here?"

"Mr. March wanted to see you, Miss Hanna," he said. "It's

just a routine matter and I'm sure he won't take much of your time."

"Hmmph," she said. "Walter Sawyer, I knew your father all of his life. If he were alive, I'm sure he would not approve of all of your associates."

I could see Walt trying to hold back a grin. "Miss Hanna," I said, "I'm aware that I offended you yesterday morning, although I assure you that was not my intention. The questions I asked you were not meant to be personal, but were merely the routine things which I have to include in my reports to my employer. But if you were offended, I apologize."

"Hmmmph," she said again, but I thought she looked a little less aggressive.

"I'd like to talk to you for just a few minutes, Miss Hanna," I continued.

"Why?" she asked bluntly. "I hear that my property has been recovered and that the person responsible for everything has gone to his just rewards."

"That seems to be true," I said. "While the insurance company apparently will not have to pay anything, the policy will still be in force, and I would consider it a favor if you'd give me a few minutes, which will help me make a complete report."

"I suppose it's my Christian duty," she said. "You may come in."

She unlocked the door and stepped inside. We followed her in. We were in a neat little living room. It was filled with fragile-looking furniture, numerous little doilies, and lace throw-pieces. It was a finicky room. Even the fireplace, in which logs were laid, was small and cramped.

"If you'll excuse me just a minute," she said. "There's a late afternoon chill these days and I like to light the fire before it sets in."

She vanished through a swinging door. As it swung open I saw she was going into the kitchen.

"This is going to be a tough one," Walt said, his voice low. "And Mrs. Singer won't be any easier."

I nodded.

She came back in with a big wad of white paper and stuffed it under the logs. She struck a match and lit it. She stood there in front of the fireplace until the logs began to crackle. Then she turned around, rubbing her hands briskly.

"I've always loved a good fire," she said. "We always had one at home when I was a girl."

"I like them myself," I said. I decided to butter her up some more. "You know, Miss Hanna, I meant to say something to you yesterday, but I didn't seem to get the chance. Those black dresses you wear—so few women are aware how smart black is. You are to be congratulated on your taste."

Well, she was part woman; she tried to hide it, but wasn't quite successful.

"How about that," she said. "The truth is, Mr. March, I don't wear black to be fashionable. I've been wearing black ever since my dear mother passed away."

"I'm sorry to hear about your mother," I said. "When did it happen?"

"Next Wednesday," she said, "it will be fifteen years since my beloved mother left me."

That stopped me. I tried to think of something to say, but she saved me the trouble.

"But you didn't come to hear about my cares," she said. "What did you want to know, Mr. March?"

"We waited quite a while," I said, trying to think of the best way to tackle her. "Where were you this afternoon?"

Her mouth tightened. "I was to a club meeting this afternoon. When that was over, Mr. March, I went to your hotel to see you."

That one caught me right between the eyes. "To see me? Why?"

"To ask you," she said forcefully, "why you don't go back where you came from and leave all of us alone."

"I don't understand," I said.

"I think you do. My possessions have been recovered and your company is not required to pay out one cent. In spite of this, in spite of the fact that you no longer have any business in Athens, you were around this morning asking questions about me of my friends. You have no right to pry into my life and make insinuations. My life is an open book, and as for the insinuations, there are laws about that."

"I made no insinuations, Miss Hanna," I said. "As for the questions, that was merely part of my job. If there had been no murder or theft, I would still have asked those same questions. When anything is insured for a large amount of money, the insurance company likes to know all about the policy holders and about the people owning the objects which are being insured. It's routine."

"Well, I don't call it proper. And that is why I called on you at your hotel."

"Sorry, Miss Hanna," I said. "I'll soon be gone."

"Well, ask your questions and leave me alone."

"Did you know Fred Swanson?" I asked.

"I knew him," she said, biting off each word. "I knew him for a drunken sot and a worthless man."

"You knew him well?"

"Better than I wanted to."

"If he stole the things originally, do you have any idea why he took things belonging only to you and Enoch Drake?"

"I don't know about that Enoch Drake—he was no better than Fred Swanson. But I expect Fred took my things out of spite."

"Why?"

"Because I objected to his being hired as the guard. I knew then that nothing would be safe. And I was right."

"Well, you have them safely back now," I said.

"No thanks to anyone except the good Lord."

"By the way," I said, "you and Mrs. Singer are related, aren't you?"

"Not so close," she said. "We're fourth half-cousins."

"What exactly was your relation to Hiram Hanna?"

"He was my great-great-grandfather."

"Mrs. Singer's, too?"

"Yes. By his unfortunate first marriage."

"And all of those things you loaned the picture company came down through the family to you?"

"Them and other things."

"Old Hiram collected quite a few possessions," I said, "for all of being a bruiser and boozer."

She stiffened. "Hiram Hanna," she said firmly, "was not a drinking man. Nor was his father, my great-great-great-grand-father who fought in the Revolutionary War. The Hannas have always been God-fearing and law-abiding. There is no blot on the Hanna family tree."

"If there had been," I said lightly, "I'll bet everybody would have rushed in with their little brushes and scrubbed it away."

She glared at me. "Mr. March, are you a Communist?" she asked bluntly.

"Not this week," I said. "I can't stand vodka. That and not being sure how to pronounce 'Malenkov'* disqualifies me, I expect. It's a pity. I've always thought that I'd look rather dashing with a bomb in my hand."

Her mouth had tightened down until it looked like an old wound. "Mr. March, I will have to ask you to leave my house."

"Just when we were getting along so well," I murmured. "Come on, Walt."

She watched us go, an uncompromising figure in black, looking like a slightly overweight avenging angel. The door slammed behind us with a finality as we plunged once more into the rose scent.

"What do you think?" Walt asked as we got into the car.

"That Miss Hanna doesn't like me," I said promptly.

He laughed. "The old gal has a phobia on a few things

---

* Georgi Malenkov briefly succeeded Stalin as leader of the Communist Party of the Soviet Union in 1953.

which she takes pretty seriously. But so do three or four thousand other people in town."

"I know," I said. "That's my trouble—my tongue has a mind of its own. But I can only take so much of that kind of stuff and then it begins to back up on me."

"Sure," he said. "But I expect Miss Hanna's had a pretty lonely and unhappy life and that's why."

"Virginity is the curse of chastity," I said. "Okay, I'm a brute. When I get back to Denver, I'll weep copious tears for Miss Hanna. Right now, she gives me a pain in a portion of my anatomy which she would consider unmentionable."

"Mrs. Singer won't be any better."

"I know," I said. "That's why I'm staying my own sweet self. Don't worry, I'll keep it down long enough to ask her a few questions."

We turned in on Mound Street and neared the white house. I saw the figure of a woman on the street ahead of us, but didn't pay any attention until she turned in at the white gate. It was Mrs. Singer. She seemed in a hurry. I glanced at my watch. It was a few minutes past five.

"Looks like she's hurrying home to get her husband's evening meal," I said, "but I'll still bet the only thing she can cook is arsenic pie."

Walt grinned as he parked the car. We got out and went up to the house, and Walt knocked on the door. Out of the corner of my eye, I saw a window curtain flutter as she looked out.

A moment later the door opened and Mrs. Singer stood in the doorway. If anything, she looked skinnier and sourer than I remembered her—which was impossible. She wore a print dress that looked as if it had been dropped into place from a tall building as she passed beneath. In a high wind.

"What do you want?" she asked abruptly.

"Hello, Mrs. Singer," Walt said. "I brought Mr. March over because he wants to ask you a few questions. You remember Mr. March—"

"I remember him," she said.

"Well, he's writing up a final report to the insurance company and would like to ask you a few questions."

"Why?" She wasn't going to move from that doorway without the equivalent of an eviction order.

"It's just a matter of form, Mrs. Singer," I said smoothly. "We just came from talking to Miss Hanna."

"Did she tell you to come bothering me with questions?" she asked suspiciously.

"Not at all," I said. "In fact, I'm not sure she knew we were coming."

She chewed that one over. Finally she stepped back, holding the door open. "You might as well come in," she said. "If she saw you, I suppose I ought to. What did she tell you about me?"

"Not a thing," I said cheerfully as we stepped into the house. Except for slight differences, the living room was a duplicate of the one we'd just left. It was prim and neat, looking as though it had not been lived in. There was nothing to indicate that this was a house in which a man lived. I wondered if there was a special room in the house in which she confined her husband.

"Should she have told us anything?" I asked.

"Land's sake, no," she snapped. "But I know Malvyna. Her tongue is always running away with her. What do you want?"

"We were here earlier," I told her. I started to take a cigarette but thought better of it; there were no ashtrays in sight and she'd probably swoon. "Where were you, Mrs. Singer?"

"Out," she snapped. "I'd like to know why you're here. Fred Swanson's dead, isn't he?"

"Yes."

"And you got back everything, didn't you?"

"Yes."

She nodded vigorously. "I knew it," she said with satisfaction. "It's in the *Messenger*. The whole story. It says that Fred Swanson was drunk and fell down and killed himself and that Chief McArdle found all the things that had been stolen. So why are you coming around and bothering a body?"

I gave her the same story I'd given Miss Hanna.

"Just like a man," she said. "Never saw a man who could do anything right. Asking a lot of fool questions after everything is over. Go ahead and get done with it. I have to make supper for Mr. Singer."

"You haven't told us where you were this afternoon," I reminded her.

For a minute I thought she was going to refuse. "We had a club meeting early in the afternoon. Malvyna was there, too. After that I was just visiting. Not that it's any of your business."

"True," I admitted cheerfully. "What club was it?"

"The Athens Literary Circle."

I nodded. "You knew Fred Swanson, Mrs. Singer?"

"I knew him as a shiftless man."

"Did you have any objections to his being hired as the guard at the museum?"

"Why should I?" she asked. "One man is just like another."

"You know," I said, "there was one thing that puzzled me about the theft. Why do you suppose that everything that was taken belonged to Miss Hanna or Enoch Drake and none belonged to you?"

Her face seemed to fold in on itself, like a flower in full retreat. "I've got my opinion about that," she said.

"Mind telling me what it is?" I asked.

"I'm not bearing witness against anybody, but I know what I know."

"How about the fact that it was your poker that was used to kill Enoch Drake?"

"I know what I know," she repeated stubbornly.

I decided to nudge her a little more. "You think Miss Hanna had something to do with it?"

"I'm not saying anything against Malvyna," she snapped.

I took out a cigarette and put it in my mouth, but didn't light it. "You know," I said, "if it hadn't been for the discovery of Fred Swanson, there are people who might have said that the fact that none of your things were taken from the museum and that it was your poker that killed Enoch Drake made it look pretty bad for you."

She regarded me with a look of pure hatred. "I'm not interested in what people might say," she said. "People talk and hens cackle."

"You and Miss Hanna are related, aren't you?"

"Distantly."

"As I understand it, you are descended from Hiram Hanna and his first wife, and Miss Hanna is descended from Hiram and his second wife?"

"Yes."

"Hiram must have been quite a man," I said casually.

"He was a man."

"Drank a lot, didn't he?"

"There is no sin of which man is not capable."

"Two wives ..."

"There would've only been one," she said, "if that hussy, Mary Kennerley, hadn't come around, wriggling and throwing herself at him so that he walked out on my great-great-grandmother." She thought about it a minute. "Still, he was better than most. I've always thought it was the fault of that scarlet woman."

"Miss Hanna's great-great-grandmother?"

"Yes."

"How many children did his first wife have?"

"Three."

"What happened to them after she died?"

"After she was killed, they were taken by her sister. Thank the Lord for that. They were raised in good Christian homes, not like they would have been if that woman had got her hands on them."

"Are they going to put all that in the picture about Hiram?" I asked.

"They are not," she said. "I don't hold with washing all of your linen in front of the world."

"You and Miss Hanna gave your approval to the story?"

"We did."

"I understand that Mr. Hoyt is rewriting the script," I said. "Does he have to show that to you, too?"

"He'd better," she said grimly.

"You think Mr. Hoyt will submit his revision to you and Miss Hanna?"

"I don't know Mr. Hoyt," she said. "But no story about the Hanna family, by Mr. Hoyt or anyone else, will be done without consent."

"You know," I said, "if the story confined itself to Hiram Hanna and to what happened one hundred and fifty years ago, I doubt very much that you could do anything."

"There will be no such story," she said. Anger had deepened the lines in her face.

"Maybe you can bring him up on charges before the Athens Literary Circle," I said, "but that's about all. Okay, Mrs. Singer, I guess I have no more questions."

"About time," she said. "Mr. Singer's supper will be late enough as it is."

"I'm sure he will bask in the sweetness of your smile," I said dryly, "and not mind. Good day, Mrs. Singer."

She made a sound in her throat. It sounded to me as near to a snarl as any lady of uncertain years could come. Walt and I walked out. The door banged shut behind us.

"Door slamming seems to run in the family," I said. I finally lit my cigarette as we walked to the car.

"Well?" Walt asked as we climbed into the car.

"To hell with it," I said savagely.

"Where do we go now?"

"Take me back to the hotel. I'm going to take a hot shower and a big slug of brandy and try to pretend that I was never introduced to some of the people I've recently met."

"I don't get it," Walt said. "I know you don't like them, but why get yourself in such a sweat about it?"

"It's not that," I said. "I know who the murderer is, but I'll be damned if I see any way to prove it."

He gave me a quick, startled look. "Who?"

I ignored the question. I wasn't interested in playing games. Walt Sawyer was close to all these people and I suspected he might put up an argument. There was no point in having that unless I had the proof. And I didn't have any.

"I can only make a very vague guess about the motive," I said. "That point should be cleared up after the expert has examined the burned pages, but that isn't what's worrying me. I'm afraid that our murderer may not be through."

"What do you mean?"

"If we're right in assuming that the diary was an important motive in the two murders already committed," I said, "then it's about time we remembered something else. Curtis Hoyt is the one person who has read the diary, has even gone through it carefully. If the diary is dangerous to somebody, then the man whose brain contains the contents of the diary is equally dangerous."

"I never thought of that," he said.

"It just started coming to me," I said. We were only a block away from the hotel. "I want you to come up with me, Walt."

"Why?"

"We're going to have our talk with Mr. Hoyt. And he's going to tell us what's in the diary."

"Maybe he'll refuse He's been pretty coy about it."

"If he's coy this time, I'm going to ask you to arrest him. That way, he'll be safe and maybe it'll make him tell us."

"What charge?"

"You can hold him twenty-four hours for questioning without booking him," I said. "Do it that way. If things aren't better by then, we'll cook up a charge "

"Okay," he said. He grinned. "Oh, boy, would we be in trouble if we pulled that on anybody in Athens!"

"It's legal," I said. "This is your chance to act like a real tough cop if he doesn't want to talk."

He parked the car and we started into the hotel. "Speaking of being coy," he said, "aren't you going to tell me who the murderer is?"

"In good time," I grunted.

We went inside. There was no clerk in sight and the lobby was empty except for Ernesto, who was sitting in one of the chairs, staring glumly at a comic book.

"Hola, chico," I said.

He looked up and his face lost its gloom. "Don Milo," he said. He waved the comic book at me. "I cannot read this, but in the pictures this one is flying through the air all the time. Yet he has no wings or any means of flying. How is this possible?"

"I think it's an old family tradition," I told him. "Or maybe he huffs and puffs. I'm damned if I know."

"Caray!" he said. "It is a tale for women." He threw the magazine into the chair.

"He's probably just what the blond one of the cinema is looking for," I said. "Ernesto, I'd like you to meet Walt Sawyer. Of the police." I switched to English. "Walt, this is Ernesto. He is my adopted son. Unfortunately, he doesn't speak English, so you can just grunt anything at him."

"Hi, Ernesto," Walt said.

"Hiya, sweetheart," Ernesto said, in a reasonable imitation of a Hollywood character.

"I see Hoyt's been giving you more English lessons," I said. I went on to explain to him that in America men did not call each other sweetheart, except possibly on the corner of Sunset and Vine. Then, I asked, "Where is your little friend?"

"Don Curtis? He went to his room perhaps two hours ago. He said that it was necessary for him to do some work and that he would see me soon. He has not yet returned."

"Then we'll go see him. You know his room number?"

"Certainly."

We got into the elevator and rode up to the fourth floor. The operator stared at us curiously but said nothing. On the fourth floor we walked down the corridor until Ernesto indicated a door. I knocked on it.

The door opened. Police Chief McArdle looked out at us.

"How did you know—" he began.

"We don't," I said, "but I can guess. Hoyt?"

He nodded. He opened the door wider and we walked into the room.

"The boy—" the Chief started to say.

"It's all right," I said. "He's my adopted son."

Ernesto caught sight of what was on the floor and cried out.

I realized I should have warned him, but I'd forgotten for the moment that he couldn't understand what we were saying. I could see him blinking to keep back a rush of tears as he turned and fired questions at me.

"I don't know yet, Ernesto," I interrupted. "I will tell you as soon as I can. I am sorry."

"He was a good friend," Ernesto said.

"So you were right, Milo," Walt said.

"What's that?" the Chief asked quickly. "Right about what?"

"Milo was just saying that Hoyt might be next."

"I'll tell you about it soon," I said in answer to the Chief's look.

I glanced around the room. In addition to Chief McArdle, there was a young man I took to be another member of his force; the Coroner; the desk clerk, looking like he was on the point of being sick; and Laslo Kryle, the Hollywood director.

Curtis Hoyt was lying in the center of the room in a crumpled heap. The back of his head was caved in. A couple of feet away, on the floor, there was a portable typewriter. From where I stood, it seemed to be bent. I could see a smear of blood and hair on it.

"Who found him?" I asked.

"Mr. Kryle here," the Chief said.

"How long ago?" I asked.

"About a half hour ago."

I looked at my watch. It was twenty minutes past six.

"I came to see him about the script," Laslo Kryle said. "We have finished our other work here and I wanted to know when he expected to complete his revision. He had insisted that he had to complete it here. I was anxious to return to Hollywood. The door to his room was not completely closed, and when there was no answer to my knock, I looked in."

I nodded and turned back to the Chief. "Any guess yet as to when he was killed?"

"Ben thinks he was killed sometime between four and five o'clock. He can't make it much closer than that."

"I know that," I said. I looked at the Coroner. "Does the Coroner also claim that Hoyt's death is accidental? That perhaps he slugged himself in the back of the head with his typewriter?" I knew that I was taking out on the Coroner an anger which I felt at myself for not having prevented this one, but I didn't give a damn.

The Coroner squirmed under my gaze. "It would appear to be murder," he murmured.

"That's broad-minded of you," I said. "I suppose the weapon was the typewriter?"

"Yes."

"It happened between four and five?"

"Yes."

"Not before four?"

"It couldn't have been much before four," the Chief said. "We know from the desk clerk here that Mr. Hoyt came up to his room about a quarter to four."

"About?" I asked, looking at the clerk.

"I think it was a quarter to four," the clerk said. He sounded nervous. "It might have been five minutes later, but no more than that."

"Okay," I said. "Did Mr. Hoyt make or receive any telephone calls after he went to his room?"

"No, sir."

"Any phone calls before, while he was out?"

"No, sir."

"How about visitors?"

"None, sir."

"Before or after?"

"No, sir."

I glanced at the Coroner. "Do you think we can say that he was killed between ten minutes to four and five o'clock?"

"Guess so," he said.

"I know you can't be certain about this," I said, "but could you make a guess about in what part of the seventy minutes the murder took place?"

He thought and fiddled with his fingers. "Maybe about the middle part of it."

"In other words, about twenty or twenty-five minutes past four?"

"About that, maybe."

"What would be your basis for that guess?"

"Well," he said uncertainly, "there ain't very much. I think rigor mortis has started to set in, in the eyelids, but there's no sign of it in the jaw muscles. But you know that ain't accurate in minutes."

"I know," I said. "It can vary an hour one way or the other. But let's say that you'd guess the murder happened about twenty or twenty-five minutes past four."

"I said I'd guess so."

I thought about it a minute. It had been just about twenty past four when Miss Hanna arrived home. And it had been a few minutes past five when we saw Mrs. Singer arriving home.

I walked across the room and bent over to look at the typewriter. It was lying on its side where it had obviously fallen. It was bent in several places and looked as if the roller was loose. There was a lot of blood and hair on the typewriter and a few threads caught in it. I looked up.

"Have you checked this yet for prints?" I asked.

"Yeah," the Chief said. "Bill, here, went over it. Ain't no prints on it except Mr. Hoyt's."

I stood up and looked at Walt. "At least one thing fits into the pattern I mentioned."

"What's that?"

"One thing that always stands out in murders committed by people who are mentally unbalanced is that they improvise so far as weapons go. We certainly have that here. The poker, which was part of the exhibit, was used to kill Enoch Drake. The andiron from the fireplace was used to kill Fred Swanson. And now the typewriter was the weapon."

"You mean you think the murderer is nuts?" the Chief asked.

"Something like that," I said. I looked around the room. Over against the wall, there was a long, flat table something like a desk. The typewriter had probably been there. Papers were stacked in neat piles on top of it.

"That's where Hoyt worked?" I asked.

"Worked," exclaimed the director. "Ha!"

"What's that mean?" I asked.

He strode over to the table and picked up a thick sheaf of papers bound in a cover.

"This," he said, "is the third draft of the script. He told me he was doing a major rewrite, a big thing—so what do I find when I look on his desk a few minutes ago? Exactly twelve pages have been rewritten. And that is all."

"You're sure?"

"Don't I know what I see?" he asked, glaring at me. "Writers! Bah!"

I walked over to the table and looked at it. On one side of where the typewriter must have stood, there was a pile of untouched paper. On the other side was a much smaller stack of papers. I glanced through this one. It was apparently twelve pages, with a carbon for each, of a fourth revision of the screenplay.

"Maybe he has more work somewhere else in the room," I said.

"In the bathroom, maybe," Laslo Kryle said bitingly. "He wouldn't go around hiding his light under a rolling stone."

"But a hit in the head isn't better than two in the bush leagues," I said. I turned to the Chief. "What about that expert?"

"He'll be here tomorrow afternoon."

"Okay," I said. "Go ahead. I won't get in your hair anymore."

"What are you going to do, Milo?" Walt asked.

"I'm going off and sulk," I said. "I'll see you later. Come on, Ernesto."

We left the room. I could see that Ernesto was still struggling with his sorrow. I put my arm around his shoulders and we walked back to our own rooms. When we were there, I poured myself a good stiff drink of brandy. I needed it.

"He was my friend," Ernesto said. "My first new friend in America."

"I know, Ernesto," I said gently.

He looked up and his black eyes were hot with unshed tears. "Don Milo, may I have my knife again?"

"No, Ernesto," I said. "We do not handle things that way in America."

"Que hemos de hacer?"

"We'll do something, Ernesto," I said. "I promise you that. Now I'd like you to tell me everything that you and Curtis Hoyt did today."

"We had breakfast together," he said. "Then we went over to the university to a building where there were many books. Millions of them. He found for me a book in Spanish and then he went through many books himself. We were there until noon."

"Did he tell you what he was doing there?"

"He said something to do with a story he was writing."

"All right. What then?"

"We had lunch and then went to some building where there were many women. Don Curtis told me it was some sort of meeting. I do not remember what sort."

I suddenly remembered hearing about a meeting early that afternoon. "Was it the Athens Literary Circle?" I asked.

"Oh, yes, that was it."

"What were you and Hoyt doing there?"

"Don Curtis made a speech to the women. I told him it was of foolishness to talk to women, but he did it."

"Did he tell you what the speech was about?"

"Only that they had asked him to tell them how he got ideas for his stories and that he was going to tell them about a new one he was writing. He seemed to enjoy making the speech very much. All the time he was talking, he seemed to be wanting to laugh."

"And the women, did they enjoy it as much?"

He shrugged. "Who knows what women enjoy, Don Milo? Perhaps some did and others did not."

"Did he tell you anything about the new story?"

"He told me how it was called, but I do not remember. He said it was a story of murder, but that was all."

"Was the title *As Old as Cain?*"

"I believe that was how he called it."

"Go ahead. What did you do after the speech?"

"We went for ice cream. Don Curtis was helping me to discover all of the flavors of ice cream in America. I had never known so many existed. It is truly a land of miracles. And Don Curtis was in very good humor. He laughed much and talked much while we had the ice cream."

"What about?"

"Mostly about Spain. He was telling me of his first visit to Spain and of when he went to the bullfight."

"What did you do next?"

"Came back to the hotel. Don Curtis told me he had to work and he went upstairs. That was the last time I saw him before I saw him there on the floor. Señor Death is a busy visitor, but he should have stayed away from Don Curtis."

There didn't seem to be much there to help me. "Look, Ernesto," I said. "Did Don Curtis ever tell you anything else about his new story? Think hard, *chico*. It may be important."

His old man's face wrinkled with concentration. "There is nothing, I think, that will help you. He said something yesterday, but it was not important."

"It might be," I said. "Try to tell me exactly what he said."

"He said, 'There goes a great story. It will get me an award.' That was all, Don Milo."

"What did he mean by 'there goes'?"

"We had gone to the post office to mail an envelope. It was a big one. He said this as I put it through the little slot for him."

"He must have been mailing the story, or a copy of it," I said to myself. "Do you know where he was mailing it?"

"No."

"Was it heavy, the envelope?"

"Pretty heavy. It was perhaps this thick." He used his thumb and forefinger to indicate approximately an inch.

"Do you know if he sent it air mail?"

He shrugged.

"Did you see the stamps? Did any of them have pictures of airplanes on them?"

"I think so, but I cannot be sure."

I thought about it. There was only one thing I could think of that it meant, but I had to admit that I might be indulging in wishful thinking. There was only one way to find out.

I picked up the phone and put in a call to Hollywood. First I called someone I knew on the Los Angeles police force. From him I got a name and a phone number and a promise to put in a good word for me if necessary. Then I made my second call to Hollywood. This time it took me a little longer, but the man I was talking to finally agreed to do what I was asking.

"*Qué hay?*" Ernesto asked when I hung up.

"I think," I said, "that everything may be all right by tomorrow morning."

The phone rang. I picked up the receiver. It was Walt Sawyer.

"We're through up in the room now," he said. "The Chief and I are down in the lobby and thought you might want to join us."

"Did you find out anything more?" I asked.

"No."

"I don't think I'll come down, then," I told him.

"But," he said stubbornly, "you said that you know who the murderer is. I have remembered myself how someone said that Hoyt would *never* do a story without consent. That was pretty strong in light of what had already happened. We'd better do something."

"If you and the Chief do what I think is in your mind," I said, "the whole town is apt to be down around your ears. You have no proof. We don't even have the motive, in spite of what was said. If you make an arrest too soon, it may do far more harm than good."

"But—" he began.

"I know what you're going to say," I cut in. "But I don't think there will be any more murders. Certainly not tonight. I have no right to give any orders to the Athens police, but I'd suggest no matter what you feel about it, don't go arresting anybody tonight. You might even make a mistake and you can be sued for false arrest."

"What do we do?" he demanded. "Sit around and wait until somebody else is killed?"

"No," I said. "I think I will have the complete motive by morning. I think also there is some little proof. But if we have the motive, I think that will be our main need. I'll be in the Chief's office in the morning and we can go ahead immediately. I'm not sure what time, but it'll be early."

"Okay," he said finally. "We'll see you in the morning, Milo." He hung up and I put the receiver back.

"Qué dijo él?" Ernesto asked.

I told him what we'd talked about.

"Could it not be a mistake to wait?" he asked. "Time is a hard master. Don Curtis was my friend."

"Note apures, chico: hombre prevenido nunca fue vencido," I said. *"A man who is prepared was never defeated."*

INT. LOG CABIN—AFTERNOON

207 MEDIUM SHOT MARY

and her four children in the cabin. The children are playing on the floor.
MARY finishes washing the dishes. She carries the dishpan to the back
door of the cabin and throws the water out.

208 ANOTHER ANGLE

as MARY turns to look at the children playing on the floor. The bitterness
in her face softens as she looks at them.

> MARY

> Matthew.

MATTHEW looks up as his mother calls to him.

> MATTHEW

> What, Ma?

> MARY

> Take the young'uns and see if you can find any blackberries on
> the back hill.

MATTHEW doesn't want to go, but he recognizes the order in his mother's voice. He gets a small bucket and leads his three-year-old brother

and two-year-old sister out of the cabin.

209 ANOTHER ANGLE

as MARY picks up the baby and puts her in the trundle bed. THE CAMERA FOLLOWS as MARY goes to the desk and takes out her diary. CAMERA MOVES IN CLOSE as she begins to write.

DIARY August 6, 1807

This morning I told Hiram about the preacher coming to the university and told him we had to get married for the sake of the children. He only laughed and went off to trade land with Abner West. I know it ain't the land. He's more interested in Priscilla West. I would rather my children were orphans than that they should have the shame of knowing we was never married. Hiram will be home soon. May God forgive me for what I'm going to do.

210 MEDIUM SHOT MARY

as she puts away the diary. She walks across the room and opens the front door to look out. She sees Hiram coming. She closes the door and hurries across the cabin to where there is a rifle. She picks it up and makes sure it's loaded. Then she turns, holding the rifle, and faces the door. She waits.

SIX

Ernesto and I were up early the next morning. As soon as we had breakfast, we went down to the Western Union office on Union Street. They were just opening. I explained that I was expecting a very long collect night letter from Los Angeles and asked them to make sure there would be no delay by sending through word to the Los Angeles office that I was there and ready to pay for it.

We had to wait almost an hour, but then one of the machines started clacking and the girl said it was for me. It clacked and clacked and they all began looking at me as if I'd just arrived from Mars. The manager started a girl counting the words.

When it was finally added up, the bill was a little more than two hundred dollars. The manager looked relieved when I counted out the money for him.

I glanced at enough of the message to be sure of the essence. Then I phoned the Chief of Police.

"We've been waiting for you," he said patiently.

"I'll be there right away," I said. "I think we're in business. Do you suppose you could get the desk clerk from the hotel up there? The one that was on duty yesterday afternoon?"

"Reckon I can," he said. "We'll be ready for you, Milo."

When I'd hung up, I took Ernesto into the first place that served ice cream. While he ate it, I read the night letter more carefully. It had more in it than I'd expected. Ernesto and I finished at about the same time. We walked up the street and turned down to the police station.

When we went into the office, the Chief and Walt were waiting with the desk clerk from the hotel.

"What the devil is that?" Walt asked as he caught sight of the sheaf of yellow telegraph forms in my hand.

"A telegram," I said, grinning.

"Looks like it ran a little more'n ten words," the Chief said dryly.

"These," I said, lifting the top half of the sheets, "are the missing pages from the rewrite on the screenplay. Hoyt did write more than twelve pages. The murderer destroyed the originals, but the carbons had been mailed. In them I think we'll find most of the missing parts of the diary. There are two pages of the script on which diary entries are shown, and I suspect they are taken verbatim from the real diary. You might call this Exhibit A. The other pages represent the outline of an original story which Curtis Hoyt was writing. It's a murder story. The murderer, under a different name, of course, and the motivation that we have here are reproduced in the story almost exactly. About the only thing missing is that the author didn't foresee that he was also going to be a victim. It seems to be an insight which, unfortunately, most victims lack."

"Where did you get those?" Walt asked.

"We can thank Ernesto," I said, "although I should have thought of it myself. He told me that he was with Hoyt the other day when he mailed something which was obviously a manuscript. I suddenly realized that Hoyt would normally register his work with the Screen Writers Guild in Hollywood. I phoned one of the officers of the guild. He promised to go down to the office and see if anything had been sent in by Hoyt. If it had, he would open the sealed envelope and send the contents to me by Western Union. Hoyt had and he did. Hoyt had sent in the carbon of the revised pages and the carbon of his original story. The murderer destroyed the originals and thought that's all there was."

"Let's get busy, then," Walt said. "Mrs. Singer—"

The door opened and a cop looked in.

"Sorry, Chief," he said. "Miss Malvyna Hanna is out here and demanding to see you at once."

"She'll have to wait," the Chief said.

"Let her come in," I said. "Maybe she has to get something off her chest."

"Okay," the Chief said.

The cop withdrew, leaving the door open. A moment later, Miss Hanna came sailing in. Her face was set in grim determination. Her gaze swept over all of us and came to rest on the Chief.

"I'm glad that man is here, Chief McArdle," she said. "It will make your task easier."

"What task is that, Miss Hanna?"

"I demand that you arrest that man," she said, pointing to me.

The Chief looked startled. "Why?"

"Yesterday," she said, "I asked this man point-blank if he was a Communist. Instead of giving me a direct answer, he passed it by making what he seemed to think was a humorous remark. I was not satisfied, so this morning I saw it as my duty to telephone friends of mine in Washington. I learned—not to my surprise, I might add—that two years ago all the leading newspapers carried stories about Mr. March being a member of the Communist Party."*

"Don't see no reason for arresting him," the Chief said mildly. "Might even be some kind of mistake." He looked at me uncertainly.

"There's no mistake," I said. "Two years ago I did a job for the State Department. The preparation for the job included forging membership in the Communist Party for me and releasing that information to the press at the right time."

"Seems like that's all there is to it," the Chief said. "Good day, Miss Hanna."

Her mouth tightened. "I'm not leaving here until something is done about that man."

"Good," I said. "I was about to suggest, Chief McArdle, that Miss Hanna remain."

"Why?" he asked.

"There is a small matter of three murders," I said. "Miss Hanna did them with her own little hands."

"Well, I never!" exclaimed Miss Hanna.

"But I thought—" began Walt Sawyer.

"I know what you thought," I said. "The other lady has a lot of hostility, but that is all. In fact, in view of the obvious competition, she would have gained by everyone's knowing about the contents of the diary. Both ladies to some degree are

---

* See *No Grave for March* by M.E. Chaber.

living in the past, but only Miss Hanna felt she had to keep part of the past a secret at any cost."

"I am not going to stay here and be insulted in this manner," she said. She headed for the door.

"Miss Hanna," the Chief said, "looks like maybe you'd better stay."

She stopped and swung jerkily around to face the room again. She looked at me, her face contorted with suppressed rage.

"Go ahead, Milo," the Chief said.

"The cause of our three murders," I said, "goes back a hundred and fifty years to Hiram Hanna and Mary Kennerley, the great-great-grandmother of Miss Hanna."

"Stop him," Miss Hanna said hoarsely. She was breathing fast as though she had been running. "You can't let him say it. You can't."

"Better keep quiet, Miss Hanna," the Chief said.

"The essence of it," I said, "is that Hiram Hanna never married Mary Kennerley, although she had four children by him and although he apparently promised her marriage many times. Finally she decided that he had no intention of marrying her and that he was becoming interested in another woman. So she killed Hiram Hanna. It went on the record as suicide, but the diary gave the truth."

Miss Hanna groaned and dropped into a chair. Her face worked convulsively.

"There are two pages of the revised script," I said, "on which Hoyt used what I'm sure we'll discover are excerpts from the diary. On one page, the new page 123, he included a part from the diary where Mary Kennerley had made up her mind what she would do, but also used action which I'm certain she set down later in the diary. By action, I mean killing. Obviously, the reason Hoyt was being so secretive about the diary and this revision was that he knew Miss Hanna would not agree to it and he hoped to somehow push it through anyway.

"I also think," I continued, "that when Enoch Drake was murdered, Hoyt correctly guessed who did it and why. From this he built his original story, which I have here—and his story is about a woman who commits a murder in modern times to conceal the fact that her great-great-grandmother had committed murder. I guess he felt that Miss Hanna would not sue. He was right."

"All this was in the diary?" the Chief asked.

"I'm sure of it," I said. "When the expert examines the burned pages, I think we will see that Hoyt used almost every step that Mary Kennerley recorded."

"Funny none of it ever came out," Walt said. "Even the professor, and he's a student of that period, believed the suicide."

"It's possible," I said, "that this diary had gone unread for one hundred and fifty years until Mr. Hoyt opened it. I know that Enoch Drake admitted that he'd never looked at it. Very possibly his father was no more curious. It might have remained uncovered forever if somebody who was nosy hadn't come along."

"How'd Miss Hanna find out what was in the diary?" Walt asked.

"I'm not certain," I said. "I can see three possibilities. It's possible that Miss Hanna knew the information all along and guessed it would be in the diary. She may have had a chance of briefly seeing the diary when it was loaned to the movie company. Or—and this would be my guess—Hoyt may have asked questions or made remarks which tipped her off. You'll have to ask her."

The Chief glanced at Miss Hanna and apparently changed his mind about questioning her just then. He turned back to me.

"Miss Hanna," I said, "is very concerned about the spotlessness of her ancestors. She even tried to deny the fact that Hiram Hanna drank heavily. This, of course, was more serious. She didn't lose much time. She soon found that there was a brief period every night when Enoch Drake was alone. She went there, waited for Fred Swanson to leave, then entered. I imagine the poker was an inspiration of the moment, chosen partly because it belonged to Mrs. Singer and might cast suspicion on her. She killed Enoch and cut off the alarms—she had been there often enough to know where they were, probably even asked out of concern for her property. She took the diary and enough other things, including things of her own, to hide the fact that the diary was what was wanted. I noticed that she usually carries a bag large enough to hold everything that was taken. She put them in the bag and left. The whole thing probably took no more than ten minutes, even though it sounds complicated."

"You got proof for this?" the Chief asked.

"Not for this," I said. "I'm reconstructing, but I'm sure it's right. I'm also guessing when I say that I think Fred Swanson later remembered that he saw Miss Hanna out on the street. He thought he could turn it to advantage and tried to blackmail her. All he knew was that he saw her under suspicious circumstances, but she had no way of knowing that was all he knew. When he contacted her, probably by phone, she agreed to meet him that night at his house. She made the appointment for late enough so there was little chance of her being seen. She intended to remove another threat, so she took with her the objects she had taken from the museum.

"Once she was there, she again improvised, using the andiron to kill him. She set the scene to look like suicide, tore out the important pages in the diary and burned them, left everything, and went back home. You may remember, Walt, we wondered why the murderer would leave all these valuable things when he could never get them back. Well, she could get part of them back, for they belonged to her.

"Now," I said cheerfully. "Next step. Shortly after lunch today, Curtis Hoyt spoke to the local literary society. Out of some kind of sadism, he told them about this original story he'd written. I imagine that he told it so Miss Hanna would know what he was talking about, but the others didn't. So she knew she had to get rid of him. She came to the hotel and waited until she saw Hoyt go to his room. She followed him up. It would be easy to do it without being seen. And again she improvised, using the typewriter as the death weapon. She then gathered up the harmful pages of the revision and the original story, stuffed them into her bag, and left. Here she was smart. She thought somebody might have seen her in the hotel and she wanted to cover that."

I turned to the desk clerk. "What time did Miss Hanna stop and ask for me?"

"About ten after four, I think," he said.

"She probably made a big point about coming to see me and not being able to, didn't she?"

"Yes. She went on something about you stirring up trouble in town, but I didn't pay too much attention. Then she marched out."

"Where did she come from?" I asked.

"Why—why from the street, I suppose."

"But you didn't actually see her walk in from the street?"

"No," he said. "No, I didn't."

"She could have come down the stairs?"

"Yeah, she could have. The stairs are right by the desk. Come to think of it, she did seem to bob up in front of me awfully quick."

I nodded. "She then walked home to find Walt and me waiting for her. She was a little upset at first, but she quickly recovered. And she was real cute. Walt," I said, turning to him, "remember when she made a point of lighting the fire?"

He nodded.

"She used Hoyt's papers to start the fire. I noticed she was using crumpled-up typewriter paper and wondered why. That was it. It was that visit, incidentally, that convinced me Miss Hanna was the one we were looking for."

"How?" Walt asked. "She didn't sound no worse to me than Mrs. Singer did."

"Not any more unpleasant," I said. "But being unpleasant doesn't make one a murderer. As soon as I realized that the diary was the motive, I knew it had to be someone so anxious to conceal something in the past that even murder became unimportant. Miss Hanna was the only one who had a desire to rewrite history. Mrs. Singer hated Hiram Hanna, but she didn't try to clean him up. Miss Hanna insisted on doing so. But she's through now. There are too many of us who know that Hiram was murdered."

"Got any proof about this last murder?" the Chief asked. He sounded anxious.

"Yes," I said. "The proof is on the typewriter. When she used it on Hoyt, she must have snagged one of her black silk gloves on it. There are several threads on it. You'll be able to match them up and prove they came from her gloves. That and the diary pages restored by the expert ought to be enough. But I don't think you even need that. Look."

The plump old woman in the black dress was sitting in the chair crying. The tears streaked down her face, but the only sound was the gulping sobs as she drew in each breath. She was staring across the room, but I don't think she saw any of us.

"Nobody should have known," she said. "The secret was buried and they had to dig it up. Don't you see? I had to stop them before they dragged me down to their level. I had to think of my position."

"There you are," I said to Walt. "There's the cesspool I was telling you about." I turned to Ernesto. *"Ven, pronto."*

We went out of the office, leaving the three men staring at what had once been a proud woman.

"It was she?" Ernesto asked.

"It was she," I said. "Your friend is avenged, if that's the right word."

"Aquello fue horrible," he said. "What will be done to her?"

"Oh, they'll be very kind to her," I told him. "If she weren't so sick in the head, they would probably execute her at once. But as it is, I expect they will lock her up and let her cry like that for another twenty years."

We went back to the hotel. I checked with the depot and found there was a train out early that afternoon. I sent a telegram to Greta and another one to John Franklin in New York.

We went downstairs just before train time and checked out. We started across the lobby. As we passed the bar, I heard my name called. I looked in. Walt Sawyer, off duty, was sitting at the bar with Niki Holden.

"Leaving us so soon, Milo?" he asked.

"So soon?" I said. "I've been here so long I feel like an old settler. Take care of yourself, Walt." I glanced at the blonde. "And I do mean, take care."

"Have a drink with us before you leave."

"No, thanks," I said evenly. "I've had a drink with the blond bombshell."

Niki Holden looked at me, the corners of her mouth curling up. "Why, Mr. March," she said. "I didn't know you cared."

"Don't take any wooden police badges, honey," I said. I waved to Walt, and Ernesto and I went out to the waiting taxi.

SEVEN

The plane floated gently down out of the sky and landed at the Denver airport. It waddled up to one of the gates and we got out. As we came into the terminal, I saw Niels Bancroft and Greta waiting. Greta caught sight of us at the same time and came running into my arms.

When I could finally let her go, I turned to Ernesto, who was pretending to examine the ceiling. "Ernesto," I said, "this is your new mother. Greta, this is Ernesto, the pride of Madrid."

She leaned down and put her arms around him and kissed him. He submitted and when she was finished even managed to mutter, *"Le agradezco mucho su amabilidad."* He turned to look at me. "It is as I told you, Don Milo—women are full of foolishness."

"It's a foolishness I like," I told him. I turned to Greta. "He says he is already in love with you." I thought that one little lie was a good investment; later they could square off if it was still necessary.

"Milo, my boy," Niels Bancroft roared, "I'm proud of you. You did a great job, just as I knew you would."

I looked at him sourly. "You did a great job on me, too. I'm not sure I'm going to know you from now on."

"It couldn't be helped, Milo," he said. "It was just the way the cards fell. Anyway, maybe it worked out better. You've got a whacking big bonus coming, and I'm giving you two weeks off for your honeymoon instead of only one. What do you think of that?"

"I think you'll probably find some work for me to do during that two weeks," I said.

"Just to show my good intentions," he said, "Greta packed your things as well as her own and brought the car down. You're going on your honeymoon right from here, so there'll be no chance for you to get stuck."

I looked at Ernesto and back to Greta. "I'm sorry, honey. I know there shouldn't be three on a honeymoon, but—"

"Let the boy stay with me," Niels said. "Looks like a nice, quiet boy. I like boys."

"There's a little problem of communication," I said.

"Not at all," he said. "I speak a little Spanish—not as well as you."

I turned to Ernesto and explained that he had a choice of going with us on our honeymoon or spending two weeks with "Uncle" Niels. I loaded the dice a little by telling him all the nice things Niels would do for him. Niels added his assurance in faltering Spanish, and Ernesto, without even hesitating, decided to stay. He didn't want anything to do with romance.

"We'll have a great time together," Niels said.

I had an idea. I excused myself and went into one of the shops in the terminal. I bought a drum, a couple of trumpets, some firecrackers, guns with caps, and finally a big box of itching powder. I wrote some instructions in Spanish on the itching powder. Then I had everything wrapped together. I took the package out and gave it to Ernesto to take with him to Uncle Niels's.

Greta and I left. She kept wondering why I laughed until long after we were out of Denver.

EDITOR'S NOTE

Whither Ernesto?

Several online reviewers have commented that the characters Greta and Ernesto don't seem to serve any purpose in this plot. Many readers will not even know who Greta and Ernesto are, unless they have read two previous Milo March novels. In *No Grave for March* (1953), Milo helps Greta escape from East Germany to the United States, where she has lived before. In *The Man Inside* (1954) we hear nothing about Greta, but Milo meets a ten-year-old Madrid street urchin, Ernesto, who assists him in his case. At the end of the book, Ernesto tells Milo, "Someday, Señor, I will come to America and you and I will be partners again. Truly." Milo replies, "Ernesto, you do that and I'll stop working for my boss, and you and I will go into business together. Truly." Who knows what Milo, or his creator, had in mind, but Ernesto pops up in America in the very next book—*As Old as Cain*—published in the same year. Although Milo and Greta are wed at the start of this book, she does not play an active role in the plot and seems to exist only to help Ernesto enter the country legally.

In the 1958 film based on the diamond-caper novel *The Man Inside,* the character named Ernesto is not a child but a Madrid taxi driver, played by the popular English singer/

actor Anthony Newley. In the book, the Madrid taxi driver is named Bernardo.

Milo and Greta are still married at the time of *The Splintered Man* (1955), but in *The Gallows Garden* (1959) it's mentioned in passing that they have divorced. The reason? It's not possible for Milo, with a dangerous occupation taking him all over the world and with his penchant for multiple female partners, to be a husband or family man.

Although the child Ernesto vanishes after this book, a character similar to him appears in *A Lonely Walk* (1956): Achille Coniglio, a poor Italian teenager who assists Milo. These kids are among a number of boys and men befriended by Milo, favorite character types of the author's who fill the pages of the series with what reviewer Mike Grost calls "scenes of male bonding" that distinguish Milo March from most other private eyes in this fiction genre.

The Milo March coat of arms was designed in the early 1970s, after twenty books of the Milo March series had recently been reissued by Paperback Library, along with five other novels by Kendell Foster Crossen.* Ken Crossen and his wife, Marcelia W. Crossen, formed a company called Milo March, Inc. We don't know the specifics of the company's purpose, beyond promoting the Milo March properties, but the coat of arms served as a logo on stationery for several years.

The motto on it, *Sanguis Dicet,* means "Blood will tell" in Latin. It is not a traditional Latin saying but is meant to resemble a motto on a medieval coat of arms. Usually the phrase "Blood will tell" means that a person whose family possesses

---

* *Born to Be Hanged* (1973) was omitted from the Paperback Library series. The five other novels are *Abra-Cadaver, The Burned Man, Once Upon a Crime, The Lonely Graves,* and *The Tortured Path.* The first four feature insurance investigator Brian Brett and are written as by Christopher Monig; the last features Intelligence agent Kim Locke and is written as Kendell Foster Crossen.

some criminal trait will eventually display it as well. Here it's a play on words suggesting that the blood of the murdered person will betray who the murderer is. It may hint that the victim speaks from the grave through the evidence and clues left behind. Blood actually has spoken, since the 1980s, through DNA profiling.

Blood Will Tell has been used several times as a book title. The first time was a serialized Hercule Poirot novel by Agatha Christie (published in 1952 as a book titled *Mrs. McGinty's Dead*). After the Milo March era, there were a few true-crime accounts and murder mysteries with that title.

One of the quadrants of Milo's coat of arms is a question mark, a symbol of mystery. Ken Crossen used to wear a silver ring with a rectangle of onyx bearing a silver question mark.

Although Milo's corporation did not survive long, the logo was definitely not a blot on his escutcheon.

Kendra Crossen Burroughs

ABOUT THE AUTHOR

Kendell Foster Crossen (1910–1981), the only child of Samuel Richard Crossen and Clo Foster Crossen, was born on a farm outside Albany in Athens County, Ohio—a village of some 550 souls in the year of this birth. His ancestors on his mother's side include the 19th-century songwriter Stephen Collins Foster ("Oh! Susanna"); William Allen, founder of Allentown, Pennsylvania; and Ebenezer Foster, one of the Minute Men who sprang to arms at the Lexington alarm in April 1775.

Ken went to Rio Grande College on a football scholarship but stayed only one year. "When I was fairly young, I developed the disgusting habit of reading," says Milo March, and it seems Ken Crossen, too, preferred self-education. He loved literature and poetry; favorite authors included Christopher Marlowe and Robert Service. He also enjoyed participant sports and was a semi-pro fighter in the heavyweight class. He became a practicing magician and had a passion for chess.

After college Ken wrote several one-act plays that were produced in a small Cleveland theater. He worked in steel mills and Fisher Body plants. Then he was employed as an insurance investigator, or "claims adjuster," in Cleveland. But he left the job and returned to the theater, now as a performer: a tumbling clown in the Tom Mix Circus; a comic and carnival barker for a tent show, and an actor in a medicine show.

In 1935, Ken hitchhiked to New York City with a typewriter under his arm, and found work with the WPA Writers' Project, covering cricket for the *New York City Guidebook*. In 1936, he was hired by the Munsey Publishing Company as associate editor of the popular *Detective Fiction Weekly*. The company asked him to come up with a character to compete with The Shadow, and thus was born a unique superhero of pulps, comic books, and radio—The Green Lama, an American mystic trained in Tibetan Buddhism.

Crossen sold his first story, "The Aaron Burr Murder Case," to *Detective Fiction Weekly* in September 1939, but says he didn't begin to make a living from writing till 1941. He tried his hand at publishing true crime magazines, comics, and a picture magazine, without great success, so he set out for Hollywood. From his typewriter flowed hundreds of stories, short novels for magazines, scripts radio, television, and film, nonfiction articles. He delved into science fiction in the 1950s, starting with "Restricted Clientele" (February 1951). His dystopian novels *Year of Consent* and *The Rest Must Die* also appeared in this decade.

In the course of his career Ken Crossen acquired six pseud-onyms: Richard Foster, Bennett Barlay, Kent Richards, Clay Richards, Christopher Monig, and M.E. Chaber. The variety was necessary because different publishers wanted to reserve specific bylines for their own publications. Ken based "M.E. Chaber" on the Hebrew word for "author," *mechaber.*

In the early '50s, as M.E. Chaber, Crossen began to write a series of full-length mystery/espionage novels featuring Milo March, an insurance investigator. The first, *Hangman's Harvest,* was published in 1952. In all, there are twenty-two Milo March novels. One, *The Man Inside,* was made into a British film starring Jack Palance.

Most of Ken's characters were private detectives, and Milo was the most popular. Paperback Library reissued twenty-five Crossen titles in 1970–1971, with covers by Robert McGin-nis. Twenty were Milo March novels, four featured an insur-ance investigator named Brian Brett, and one was about CIA agent Kim Locke.

Crossen excelled at producing well-plotted entertainment with fast-moving action. His research skills were a strong asset, back when research meant long hours searching library microfilms and poring over street maps and hotel floorplans. His imagination took him to many international hot spots, although he himself never traveled abroad. Like Milo March, he hated flying ("When you've seen one cloud, you've seen them all").

Ken Crossen was married four times. With his first wife he had three children (Stephen, Karen, Kendra) and with his second a son (David). He lived in New York, Florida, Southern California, Nevada, and other parts of the country. Milo March moves from Denver to New York City after five books of the series, with an apartment on Perry Street in Greenwich Village; that's where Ken lived, too. His and Milo's favorite watering hole was the Blue Mill Tavern, a short walk from the apartment.

Ken Crossen was a combination of many of the traits of his different male characters: tough, adventuresome, with a taste for gin and shapely women. But perhaps the best observation was made in an obituary written by sci-fi writer Avram Davidson, who described Ken as a fundamentally gentle person who had been buffeted by many winds.